1

BOOK 1 IN THE

CALMATZA SERIES

ELISA JOHNSON

Other books by Elisa Johnson:

The Three Masks (2016)

TABLE OF CONTENTS

PROLOGUE

Welcome to Corvate Manor, the home of 57-year-old Victoria Corvate, who is probably the wealthiest woman on the entire planet of Calmatza, thank you very much. With a total of 7,043 Sentus, she ranks second in wealth. Well, that's not the point.

"Excuse me!! Talking about my age in public and saying I'm not important!"

Sorry Mrs. Corvate!

Anyway, the point is the servant girl who works there. She has a very interesting secret that she will never tell Mrs. Corvate and her horrid son, Matthew.

This servant girl was once a baby who was left on a hilltop by her father. At least that's what she thinks.

She thinks her family might be the Serventsas. The Serventsas are the royal family of Grystall, a town opposite from Mrs. Corvate's hometown, Yellaburg.

She doesn't have any of her family's fortune except a medallion in the shape of a flower.

It is said that Queen Shirley Serventsa wore a medallion in the shape of a rose. That is her only memory of her long lost family. The people of Yellaburg found her on the hilltop and took her to Yellaburg on Mrs. Corvate's private glider, the Blood Glider. Yellaburg was the sworn enemy of Grystall. That's why nobody wanted her.

Finally, after taking seven years to decide what to do, the people sent her to live as a temporary servant for Mrs. Corvate. This is a secret she will never ever forget.

CHAPTER 1

RAE'S LIFE

This servant girl's name is Rae. She has no other name. She is a twenty-five-year old who can be very secretive. She's been a servant of Mrs. Corvate's for eighteen years now and is very tired of it.

Mrs. Corvate called her Matthew's private servant, but Rae did not have to do things just for Matthew. She also had to make supper, wash dishes, sweep floors, do the laundry and set up for dinner parties.

Rae found that being Matthew's private servant was helpful when it came to education. Whenever his private tutor came on weekends, Rae would always be there. She learned to read and write and do arithmetic over the last eighteen years.

Mrs. Corvate had many dinner parties. Rae didn't like it. She hated it when she had to stand by the dining room door and be as silent as a mouse.

She hated it even more when Mrs. Corvate made her organize everything. She had to clean the entire parlor all by herself, including the polishing, the dusting, the scrubbing, and cleaning out the fireplace.

"Another dinner party?" asked a servant named Charley.

"Yes, and I want a *real* tablecloth," answered Mrs. Corvate. Then she started muttering about her last dinner party when Charley had put Matthew's bed sheets on the parlor table instead of the tablecloth. Rae well remembered that last dinner party. No one could forget it.

THE LAST DINNER PARTY

As usual, the butler, Timothy, answered the door.

Vanessa Garden entered the huge mansion. Benjamin and Mary Garden walked slowly behind their mother.

"It's great to see you again, Victoria," Mrs. Garden exclaimed and hugged Mrs. Corvate, as if she hadn't seen her in a long time.

"Come to the parlor," Mrs. Corvate responded as she led the family into the freshly cleaned (by Rae) parlor.

The parlor lamps were dim because Mrs. Corvate liked darkness. The white tablecloth stood out.

"I must say, Victoria, I don't recall you making a tablecloth like that."

Mary didn't say it, but she thought her patchwork was prettier than Mrs. Corvate's tablecloth.

When Mrs. Corvate looked closely, she saw that it was not her

TABLECLOTH AT ALL. IT WAS MATTHEW'S BED SHEETS.

THE BOYS WERE OUTSIDE PLAYING, SO THEY DID NOT NOTICE, BUT MRS. CORVATE HAD NEVER BEEN MORE EMBARRASSED IN HER LIFE.

Ever since that dinner party, Mrs. Corvate had to remind Charley to put the real tablecloth on the parlor table.

"Rae, get to work!" yelled Mrs. Corvate. Rae had been so lost in thought that she looked like she was sunbathing in the fireplace.

"Yes, madam," answered Rae.

"India!" Mrs. Corvate called in a demanding voice.

India was the horse girl and was only eighteen. She became a servant when she was eleven and Rae was eighteen. Her clothes were usually covered in dirt. On certain days she disappeared from the stable. No one knew where she went. She had a pretty interesting story about how she became a servant, but hers was too ordinary to be kept a secret.

India was an orphan. She never knew her mother. She lived in Florei happily until scarlet fever struck and killed her father. India was only nine years old when she had to be sent to live at Eastern Floreian Orphanage.

India stayed there until she was eleven. Finally, the orphanage lost its money and couldn't afford to care for all the children. Some of the children were adopted into new families, but Mrs. Corvate tricked the ones who weren't into becoming servants.

India was one of the people she tricked. Luckily, she could read and write. She had gone to school in Florei. Charley and Timothy became servants that way too.

Twenty-seven-year-old Marilyn, Mrs. Corvate's best friend and honorary daughter, was probably the most annoying person ever. She spent her time trying to get servants punished. Mrs. Corvate had found her lying on the steps of her manor when Marilyn was only nine.

Nova was Marilyn's twin, but she was a servant. When Nova was nine, she became a servant at the same time as Rae. She was now twenty-seven and Rae's only friend.

Rae looked at her handwritten schedule. It was 5:30 pm and she was on laundry duty. Mrs. Corvate kept the servants on a tight schedule. Rae would work hard all day, but she had to follow her schedule EXACTLY HOW IT WAS WRITTEN. She couldn't even go into a certain room if it wasn't on her schedule.

Rae and Nova went into the kitchen. Nova filled the washtub with water, while Rae shredded a special root that could be made into soap. Rae put the shredded root into the water. She and Nova stayed in the kitchen for an hour washing and hanging clothes, when they came across India's mucky clothes. Rae had to wash them in the river or else they would make the washtub dirty. They washed everything from servants' clothes to Mrs. Corvate's huge frilly dresses.

Mrs. Corvate believed that all of her servants should like huge frilly clothes just because she did. Rae didn't, and she hated it when Mrs. Corvate forced her to wear a gigantic dress as punishment.

"India!" yelled Mrs. Corvate, "You get over here!"

India hurried over. She was wearing new clothes that were still dusty.

"You didn't enter Ivy in the fast horse race!" she yelled.

"Ivy isn't very fast," answered India. India was a defiant servant. Rae admired her for that.

"Just the same, I want her to be in that race," Mrs. Corvate insisted. "I cannot stand for a Corvate horse to be in the *slow* horse race. Do you understand, India?"

"Yes madam," answered India, "but she'll probably come in last."

India went off to the stable to train Ivy.

"As for you, Rae," said Mrs. Corvate, looking at her with dark scheming eyes, "We will have to have a servant meeting to discuss your faults."

Rae had been in many such servant meetings before, but this time, she did not know what she had done. She was so worried that she didn't see Marilyn whispering to Grace, the delivery servant.

CHAPTER 2

A NEW FRIEND

"So, after that deliberate mistake, you deserve severe punishment!" Mrs. Corvate glared fiercely at Rae.

Rae certainly thought that Mrs. Corvate took servant meetings too seriously. She would gather the servants in rows. It was like a trial except—for some strange reason—26-year-old Matthew was the judge.

"Nova!" Mrs. Corvate yelled. "Marilyn caught Rae talking to you while you were doing laundry!"

"Madam, she didn't do it," Nova stammered. "Marilyn is just trying to find an excuse to punish Rae."

"Don't lie to me, Nova!" yelled Mrs. Corvate. "I have a group of servants who also saw Rae talk to you."

Mrs. Corvate certainly had more than a group of servants. Only Nova and India were with Rae.

Marilyn and Grace were both witnesses.

"Marilyn told me that Rae had been talking," Grace told Matthew.

Grace tried to hide it, but Rae thought Grace was trying to remember what Marilyn had told her to say.

Then Nathaniel spoke, "I heard her from the parlor."

"What did she say?" asked Matthew.

"W-well" he stammered. "I couldn't really—"

"Be quiet!" yelled India.

Everyone was surprised. India was not usually a talker. She said, "None of you heard Rae talk at all! I have a story to tell all of you who thought Rae was talking."

India paused and looked straight into Marilyn's eyes. Marilyn shivered. Even though India was the youngest of all Mrs. Corvate's servants, she was probably the most defiant. She knew it was risky, but she now had a chance to save a servant.

INDIA'S STORY

I WAS IN THE HALLWAY, DUSTING THE FURNITURE, WHEN I HEARD THE FAMILIAR SOUND OF THE LAUNDRY BEING WASHED.

I PEERED INTO THE KITCHEN, AND RAE WAS TAKING OUT MY MUCKY CLOTHES TO WASH IN THE RIVER.

THEN I SAW MARILYN. SHE WAS WHISPERING TO GRACE. I GOT CLOSE ENOUGH TO HEAR.

MARILYN WAS SAYING, "I KNOW SHE WILL HAVE A SERVANTS MEETING, SO I WANT YOU TO SAY AT THE MEETING THAT I TOLD YOU RAE HAD BEEN TALKING. DO YOU UNDERSTAND?"

"YES, MARILYN," ANSWERED GRACE.

I KNEW THAT MARILYN WANTED RAE TO GET PUNISHED, SO I FOLLOWED HER.

I HEARD HER SAY, "NOW NATHANIEL, I WANT YOU TO TELL THE OTHER SERVANTS THAT RAE WAS TALKING TO NOVA."

I KNEW THAT RAE HAD NOT BEEN TALKING AT ALL. IT WOULD HAVE BEEN IMPOSSIBLE, FOR SHE WAS STILL OUTSIDE WASHING MY CLOTHES.

"You see, madam?" asked India. "If Rae was talking to Nova, she wouldn't be outside washing my clothes."

"Do you have evidence?" asked Mrs. Corvate.

"Yes," answered India. She rummaged into Grace's delivery bag.

Inside there was a piece of paper with the words,

"Marilyn told me that Rae had been talking."

Mrs. Corvate studied the note. "How do you know that Marilyn wrote this?"

"I've noticed that Marilyn has grown to hate Rae," answered India. "I know that she would only do something like that to a person she hates."

"That doesn't prove anything," Mrs. Corvate argued.

"I admit it!" Grace suddenly shouted. "Marilyn did give us directions!"

"Grace, what are you doing?" screamed Marilyn.

Everyone was talking at once. Marilyn was scolding Grace. Nathaniel was yelling with rage, for he had been hoping that Marilyn would get her point across better. Nova was congratulating India for saving her friend, but Rae just stood there. She had no idea that India had wanted to protect her for all these years.

Rae had always been fond of India, but now she understood that Nova was not her only friend. She could be friends with India when Nova was not there. Rae also realized that India had always liked her the way she was. Maybe it would always be this way. Anyway, for now, she would have a friend to turn to when she was not with Nova.

Nothing else mattered anymore to Rae, except that she still missed her family, but she would probably never stop feeling like that.

One night in the dark servant's quarters, Rae thought about India and Nova, her two friends. She could not sleep. She crept over to India, who didn't have a mattress to sleep on. Mrs. Corvate said she didn't need one.

"India," whispered Rae. India's head flew up.

"Can we promise to be friends?" she asked. India's eyes opened very wide.

"I thought you were friends with Nova," she whispered.

"I am friends with her, but I know that you have always been fond of me."

India knew that was true and ever since, Rae and India were friends. They did their work together and tried not to pester Mrs. Corvate.

One morning, India got up earlier than the sun. She was working on a tin can telephone. It was a piece of string tied to two tin cans.

"What are you making that for?" asked Rae.

"Well, I was thinking that you could put this can in the shed while you're on shed duty, and I could put the other end in the stable. Whenever you want to talk to me, you can talk without Mrs. Corvate noticing. I attached a third one so you could talk to Nova as well. If you ever want to talk to me, just yell, 'Report India!' and I will respond."

Then a loud voice yelled, "Report India!"

"That's Nova," India explained.

"It's me, India!" she responded.

"I'm only testing it," answered Nova's voice. She clanged two spoons.

"That means the report is over," India told Rae.

Now, whenever the three friends wanted to talk, they could just pick up their cans and talk.

Rae loved it when both servants yelled, "Report Rae!" at the same time. She also loved the sound of clanging spoons.

Mrs. Corvate never saw them talking. Neither did Marilyn or Matthew, for they hated the three friends, and tried to keep their distance from them.

Rae was becoming very close with her friends. So close that maybe, just maybe, she might be able to tell them her secret.

CHAPTER 3

IDEAS

"So, let's go through the possibilities of being a Serventsa," suggested practical India.

Rae had told her friends about her secret through the tin-can telephone. "One possibility is that I have a flower medallion that might have belonged to a Serventsa," Rae told her.

Nova objected, "But maybe it didn't belong to a Serventsa. Flower medallions were in style when I ran away from home. My mother wore one herself."

Marilyn and Nova's parents brought them up poorly. Well, at least they brought Nova up poorly. The family lived in Yellaburg. The girls were taught how to run a household, how to be fine ladies, and how to dance.

They were not well educated, for their mother didn't believe that ladies should go to school. They were punished if they raced and played with the boys. It was not ladylike to run and play games.

Marilyn loved her upbringing, but Nova did not. She didn't want to grow up being a young lady who wore huge dresses all the time. She complained all the time to her mother, and when she turned nine, she ran away. Marilyn tried to find her, but soon after she did, they both fell asleep on Mrs. Corvate's steps.

Marilyn enjoyed her life immensely as Mrs. Corvate's friend. Nova preferred anything to a servant's life, but there was nothing she could do about it.

One Tuesday, Nova's mother came to the Corvate Manor. She was wearing a tulip medallion.

"They're in style these days," she told Mrs. Corvate. They talked for a while, and Nova hoped that her mother wanted her back, but she had only asked for Marilyn to have proper upbringing if she was going to spend a lot of time at Corvate Manor.

The next day, Mrs. Corvate was wearing a

poppy medallion. When Mrs. Corvate had a dinner party, Rae noticed Mrs. Corvate's friend, Edia Peterson, was wearing a water lily medallion. Soon everyone was wearing flower medallions, from sunflowers to orchids.

"You do have a point," replied Rae to her friends, "But *I* wear a rose."

"I guess you're right," sighed Nova. "I never saw anyone wear a rose medallion."

"We still don't have any proof that Rae is a Serventsa," India reminded them. "The medallion doesn't explain anything."

"Do you remember anything else?" asked Nova.

"I do remember seeing a long golden spear," answered Rae.

"That explains something," Nova told her. "Only royal guards carry spears."

"It could have belonged to Florei," India reminded her. Florei was the town between Yellaburg and Grystall.

"India does have a point, Nova," Rae told her.

"I didn't know Florei had a royal family,"

Nova said. She was beginning to feel like Yellaburg was the only town without royalty.

"It doesn't," answered India. "Golden spears from Grystall are given to people in Florei who need money. Florei is too small to have royalty."

"Then why don't we have royals?" asked Nova.

"You never had royals, Nova," answered India. "All the rich folks in Yellaburg fought over being a royal until Mrs. Corvate was the only one left. All the others fled to The Outlands."

"Wouldn't that mean Mrs. Corvate would be Queen?" asked Nova.

"No," answered India. "The Serventsas wouldn't let her."

"Let's get back to *my* being a Serventsa," suggested Rae.

Nova began asking many questions. "What was it like to be left on a hilltop? Did you ever see your father? Does anyone know if you're a Serventsa or not?"

"That's it!" interrupted India.

"What?" asked Nova.

"If we could find someone who knows something about Rae's background, she might be able to help us," answered India.

"How are we going to sneak out?" asked Rae.

"I found a secret underground passageway from the stable to my old orphanage," answered India.

"What happens when Mrs. Corvate finds out?" asked Nova.

"It's all under control," India answered simply.

"So we start tomorrow?" asked Rae.

"Six o-clock sharp," answered India.

The clanging of spoons rang out. Tomorrow would be a big day.

That night Rae could not sleep. Part of her was worried about Mrs. Corvate catching her, but all of her wanted to know if she was a Serventsa.

That evening, Nadia and Michael Ramsey were downstairs with Mrs. Corvate. Michael Ramsey was Mrs. Corvate's lawyer, and Nadia was his wife. Rae slept close to the vent, so she could hear every word they spoke.

"Yes, Ramsey, I want to send them away," Mrs. Corvate said. She sounded angry. "They're becoming friends, and I don't want them to be secretly talking."

Rae gasped. Mrs. Corvate wanted to send her away. This was the happiest night in a long time.

"India!" she whispered. "Nova!"

India always woke up when someone told her to, but Rae had to shake Nova until she woke up.

"Mrs. Corvate wants to send us away!" Rae whispered excitedly. "I heard her talking to her lawyer about us!"

"Are you sure she means us?" asked Nova.

"Who else would she be talking about?" asked Rae.

Nova looked astonished, but India looked as if she already knew that Mrs. Corvate wanted to send them away.

"India, how do you know all of this stuff?" asked Rae.

"Some people don't notice secret passageways, but I do," she answered.

"You mean—there are passageways throughout this mansion?" Nova, who had never gone to school in her life, was very surprised.

"How long will it take us to get from the stable passageway to Florei Orphanage?" asked Rae.

"About two days or so," answered India carelessly.

"Two days?" asked Rae. "We can't travel for that long without being caught."

"It's an *underground* passageway Rae," India reminded her. "I'm sure we can make it."

"What happens when we get to Florei?" asked Nova.

"The head of the orphanage, Mrs. Edwards, knew Shirley Serventsa," answered India. "She might be able to tell you if you're a Serventsa."

"We should get some sleep," suggested Nova. "We will need to get to the passageway before we have new owners."

Rae lay back on her mattress. She thought of the busy day ahead of her. She could not guess who this Mrs. Edwards was. If she knew her parents, whoever they were, she knew that they were missing her.

At least she wouldn't be a servant anymore. For the first time in her life, she would be free to do as she pleased. Maybe she would even be able to find out if she was a Serventsa or not.

CHAPTER 4

THE JOURNEY BEGINS

"This is our first direction," India announced, holding a map. The girls were in the stable trying to find the passageway. India was also holding a huge camping bag that she'd found in the stable. Who knew what was in it?

The directions were very strange. They were so strange that only India could read them:

Ψου μυστ βρινγ α σιλκ σηαωλ ανδ

χολορεδ ϖειλσ   (You must bring a silk shawl and colored veils).

"We should also bring Jet," India told Nova, pointing to the foreign letters:

Ψου μυστ τακε α τρυστωορτηψ ηορσε το Φλορει. (You must take a trustworthy horse to Florei).

And so they had to bring a horse.

"How did you learn to read this strange writing?" asked Rae.

"It's all here in *The Guide to Ancient Script*," answered India. She handed Rae a thick leather bound book. It had the whole ancient alphabet in it! A few of the letters looked the same as normal ones like the "A" and the "O", but most of the ancient letters were different from the regular ones. This is what was on the first page:

α = a	ν = n
β = b	o = o
χ = c	π = p
δ = d	θ = q
ε =e	ρ = r
φ = f	σ = s
γ = g	τ=t
η = h	υ=u
ι = i	ϖ=v
φ = j	ω = w
κ = k	ξ = x
λ =l	ψ = y
μ = m	ζ = z

"Are you sure it's safe?" asked Nova.

"Did you ever wonder where I was when Mrs. Corvate could never find me?" asked India, opening the trapdoor. "I was in this trapdoor with a few horses. I'm sure it's safe."

Jet pulled and whinnied, trying to get loose, but the rope held him right there with them.

Nova couldn't believe that India wanted to bring Jet. He kicked Nova right on the back!

"I thought you were supposed to bring a *trustworthy* horse!" screamed Nova. "Not a wild one!"

"Jet is trustworthy enough!" argued India. "You just don't know him very well!"

"I know him enough to tell you that he is not trustworthy!" screamed Nova.

"You wouldn't know; you've never ridden a horse in your life!" India was angry, and so was Nova.

Nova didn't like Jet, but Jet was India's favorite horse. He liked hanging around India too. He was a wild horse, so he didn't live in the stable.

Rae wasn't paying attention to anything Nova

and India were saying. She was too busy looking at the ancient capital letters. This is what they were:

A = A	N = N
B = B	O = O
X = C	Π = P
Δ = D	Θ = Q
E = E	P = R
Φ = F	Σ = S
Γ = G	T = T
H = H	Y = U
I = I	ς = V
ϑ = J	Ω = W
K = K	Ξ = X
Λ = L	Ψ = Y
M = M	Z = Z

The three girls started down the passageway.

"Ditch!" yelled Nova suddenly.

"Very funny, Nova," responded Rae. Rae had made up the ditch joke after the tin can telephones were made.

"No, I mean there really is a ditch!" yelled Nova.

Rae looked down and saw a deep brown ditch. It was not pitch dark, for oil lamps were lit around the passageway, but no one had seen the ditch.

"How do we get down there?" asked Nova.

India was already climbing down. Rae climbed down into the ditch carefully after her. Once they got to the bottom, Nova untied the rope that kept them from falling. She climbed down after India, trying to see where Rae was going.

India was looking at the map:

Ψουλλ φαλλ ιντο α διτχη ιφ ψου αρε νοτ χαρεφυλ. (You'll fall into a ditch if you are not careful).

"I'm glad we didn't fall into the ditch," Nova sighed. She heard Jet frisking about wildly.

India was leading him into the ditch, but he would not go. He wrenched from India's grasp, and galloped away from her!

"Whoa, Jet!" India screamed.

He would not stop. His jet-black mane and tail

flew around.

Nova and India did not realize that Rae was not there. "Where are the directions?" asked Nova.

"Forget the directions!" yelled India, "Grab Jet!"

Rae was looking at the ancient directions. She still had *The Guide to Ancient Script* with her.

At the end of the long ditch, the passageway was completely blocked off with a rock wall except for a tiny opening. It was a little cave.

Rae was in that cave at the end of the ditch.

Γιϖε τηε Σερϖεντσα σπιριτ α χερεμονψ. (Give the Serventsa spirit a ceremony).

Rae did not know what the Serventsa spirit was, but she knew how to throw a ceremony. She had seen Mrs. Corvate do it.

She knew there was a table and silverware. There was no table, so Rae scraped up some dirt and packed it until it was a little table. She took the antique silverware that India had stolen from the kitchen.

Rae was puzzled because she didn't know how to give a ceremony to a spirit. She spread her brown blanket on the "table" and sat back on her heels to look over her efforts. It did not look one bit like Mrs. Corvate's ceremonies, but it was the best she could do. She was not roped to Nova anymore, so she could move around as she pleased. Nova entered the little cave.

"You were here the whole time?" asked Nova.

"Yes, I was," answered Rae. "Where's India?" she asked.

"Trying to tame Jet," answered Nova.

"I need her right now," Rae told Nova. "I can't figure out how to give a spirit a ceremony."

Nova stared at the ratty table. "Don't count on me to know the answer," Nova told Rae. "I can't read that map. I can't even read."

India was covered in scratches when she came into the cave. Her face was red, and she had Jet on a rope. "I'm not doing that again," she gasped.

"How do you give a spirit a ceremony?" asked Rae.

India looked at Rae's efforts, and explained that the map meant to give a ceremony the ancient way.

If she hadn't thought she was a Serventsa, Rae would have thought the ceremony was too strange to be true, but Rae now realized that she would probably do more things like it on this adventure. It was much different than the ceremonies Mrs. Corvate held.

Nova just thought it was plain nonsense. She never had to dress up in veils at Corvate Manor. Then again, she wasn't at Corvate Manor. The three girls didn't think they would ever see Mrs. Corvate again.

CHAPTER 5

THE RIGHT CEREMONY

India had a demanding side. Not as demanding as Mrs. Corvate, but very close. Now was one of the times.

"Nova! Put on the veils! Rae! Hurry up with the mantel!" She exclaimed.

"I look ridiculous, India!" complained Nova. She was wearing an orange silk shawl with a green border. Colored veils were all down her arms and over her head.

"If you don't do the dance of the Ancient times, we won't have a proper ceremony," India told her.

"Can't Rae do it?" groaned Nova.

"Rae has to do the offerings," India reminded her.

"What will *you* be doing?" asked Nova.

"I have to build a stone tablet," answered India. "Now, practice your dance."

Nova wiggled her hips and put her hands in a tree pose. It was a silly dance. Rae was making a mantel for the offerings. To keep Jet still, Rae fed corn and oats to him. She looked at the map to see what the offerings were: Τηε οφφερινγσ αρε α χρεχσεντ στονε ανδ α πι εχε οφ πινεωοοδ. (The offerings are a crescent stone and a piece of pinewood).

"What kind of offering is that?" asked Rae. "An ancient one," answered India, as if this were the most normal offering in the world.

"Well, India studied for six years," thought Rae. "She would know more than I."

Rae found a patch of different stones that had fallen from the cave ceiling. She could not yet find a crescent shaped one. They were hard to locate because stones usually fell from the cave in triangles. Finally, she had built a mantel.

Nova knew that it was not proper for girls to build, but it looked so fun that she had to try it. Rae let her help until India realized that she had no one to do the Indian dance, so Nova had to do that.

Rae had built the mantel out of strong oak. She nailed a long slab into four strong logs, so it looked like a table. Then she attached a wooden frame to the oak table.

Rae then decorated the mantel. First, she painted the mantel steel blue. Then she tied the rest of the colored veils on the mantel. After that, she placed one of Mrs. Corvate's china bowls on the mantel. The bowl would hold the offerings. The statue of a galloping horse was placed on the left side of the bowl. The other statue was of Jenna Serventsa, the first queen of Grystall.

India was making a stone tablet. She had her own chisel. She took a piece of flat stone and wrote:

Φλοω

Φιερψ

Συνλιγητ

Νατυρε

Σκψ

Ωατερ

Αμετηψστ

She told Rae the words she was writing, "These are the elements of Grystall."

Rae studied the marks on the tablet; then she realized that it was ancient script.

"Is the ceremony ready yet?" asked Nova.

"We have to find the offerings," India reminded her. "I also need to practice my drumbeat."

"What will I do?" asked Nova.

"Let me see your dance," responded India. "Then you can help with the mantel."

Nova felt foolish doing the dance, but she showed India her best work. She wanted to help Rae with the mantel, so she had to do her dance properly.

India's drumbeat was a sort of chant. It almost sounded hollow. India looked at Nova for a long time before she told her she could help Rae. Nova placed the flowers below the mantel while Rae brushed the china bowl. India came over with two sticks. She had brushed them well, and cut them to be smooth around the edge.

"Use these for your hair," she told them as if it were obvious how to do your hair with a stick. Nova and Rae just stared at them. India had already done her hair.

"How do we do that?" asked Rae.

India took the stick out of her hair. She carefully went through complicated directions of how to fix your hair with a stick.

As much as India had studied, she was not very good at teaching. She had learned from her father how to do her hair with a stick. Her father had taught her well, but India had never taught before. Rae and Nova were confused. First, India had to help Rae. Then, just as Rae almost had it, Nova couldn't remember which way to wrap her hair around the stick.

India had to demonstrate again how to turn the stick to the right. They would try, but then their sticks would fall out and the whole thing would start over. India finally resolved to do their hair for them. It was uncomfortable for them, but she had to do it if Nova and Rae couldn't do it themselves. Finally, after a long while, the sticks were in.

"Now, don't let them fall out," India told them. "If they do, the ceremony will fall apart."

"Why do we have to do this?" asked Nova. "It's 1845, India; people do their hair with ribbons."

"The ancient people didn't," answered India.

"Is the ceremony ready yet?" asked Rae.

"I think so," answered India. India still thought there was something missing. She looked at the map. It read:

Μακε αν ινστρυμεντ ουτ οφ ρεδωοοδ.

(Make an instrument out of redwood).

"What do they mean by instrument?" asked Rae. India was already making it.

"That's right, leave it to India," Nova whispered to Rae. Nova was jealous because India didn't have to spend her life learning how to serve tea.

"The ceremony is ready," India announced. "Nova will start it."

Nova began to dance.

CHAPTER 6

UNFORTUNATE-ISH CEREMONY

The drumbeat rang out while Nova danced. Then the hollow sound of the instrument played. India was cunningly playing both. Rae waited for the signal to give the offerings. Rae did not say it, but she thought she saw Jet slip through the stone. He seemed to have disappeared. Nova had noticed it too.

As usual, India looked like she was expecting that to happen and gave the signal. Nova sat on the ground while Rae stepped forward. The tablet was very heavy, but the offerings were light. Rae did not know why she had to give the offerings. Why couldn't Nova or India do it?

Rae kneeled down in front of the mantel. She did not say anything because you must never talk during an ancient ceremony, but she did feel like the offerings were starting to make more sense. The pinewood was turning to gold, and the stone was transforming to silver.

The tablet turned into a violet liquid that melted over Rae's fingers. While it was a liquid, it seemed to have something solid underneath that kept the offerings from flowing away. Then, the liquid burst into many blue flames that had no temperature at all. The flames ceased and a brilliant green light shone from the offerings. Yellow leaves curled around the offerings like a bowl.

Rae placed the leaf bowl into the china one and watched. After six and a half seconds, she poured red-orange liquid into the leafy bowl. The liquid was called Grysetsa, and it summoned the Serventsa spirit.

Rae waited. When she saw the spirit haze, she gave the Grysetsa a boost with amethysts. The Grysetsa turned ruby red. The spirit had not appeared completely.

Rae tried not to look at the hazy spirit appearing. India had told her that the spirit would not see things like they are until it was at full vision. A spirit who had not fully appeared could see Rae as an evil beast or human/bird.

Suddenly, her hair seemed to drop. Rae had forgotten she had a stick in her hair. If the stick fell out, the ceremony would fall apart!

The other two started talking at once. They were trying to convince Rae to do what they thought was best.

This is what it sounded like:

Nova: "Let it fall apart! This ceremony doesn't matter to me!"

India: "If the ceremony fails, we won't get to Florei!"

Nova: "We don't need to do this ceremony!"

India: "You want to know your family, right?"

Suddenly, there was another voice. "They must have run away. We searched the whole manor and they're not there."

"Our new owner!" whispered Nova. "It's a man."

"He doesn't sound any better than Mrs. Corvate," Rae whispered. She listened a bit longer.

"He studies legends," Rae told Nova. "I heard him say that."

"He's in the stable!" India was frantic. If he studies legends, he might know about this passageway!"

"We have to finish the ceremony before he gets here!" Nova whispered.

"That's the first time she said that," India told Rae.

Rae went to the mantel after making sure her stick was securely in her hair. She poured fresh amethysts into the Grysetsa. She could still see the hazy spirit.

"Mrs. Corvate's coming!" India whispered.

"Serventsa Jenna," a voice called. The spirit was in clear vision now, "Serventsa Tina. Serventsa Abby. Serventsa Marian."

"The spirit is saying the names of the Serventsa queens," India explained. After Serventsa Emily and Serventsa Carolina, the spirit finally announced Serventsa Shirley. Then it stopped; it did not say, "Serventsa Rae."

The spirit said, "You have summoned me. I will let you through the wall if you can make this ice crack."

Nova would not touch the cold ice. She did not want her fingers to turn to ice. She did not realize that touching ice doesn't turn your fingers to ice. Even India did not know how to crack ice.

"I've done this before," Rae told India.

"You have?" asked India.

Rae replied, "Mrs. Corvate made me do it for one of my punishments. Just put it in warm water." She took a bowl of stove-heated water and dropped the ice cube in it. She held the bowl close to the spirit so the spirit could see. They waited and waited. Finally the ice made a sharp sound. There was a crack right across the middle.

"Well done, Rae. I will now let you through." The spirit was cutting into the solid wall with a silver dagger.

Either the dagger was very sharp or the stone became softer, but somehow the blade cut right through.

"There they are!" yelled a voice. Rae turned to see Mrs. Corvate and their new owner!

"Go, Rae." the spirit told her. "I'll hold them off."

Rae pulled India and Nova with her.

The spirit closed the stone leaving the two adults blocked from Rae and the other girls.

"Those girls are no longer your servants, Victoria."

Mrs. Corvate did not like being called Victoria by strangers, but she was so frightened that she did not protest.

The spirit turned to the man beside Mrs. Corvate.

"I'm Oliver Michaels," he said. "I study legends."

"You volunteered to be the owner of the girls?" asked the spirit.

"Yes uh—"

"Call me Landei."

"Well Landei, Victoria here wanted to have a rich, suitable master for the girls. She taught me how to treat them."

"I don't want a master for them that is too harsh," Mrs. Corvate told Landei.

The girls had been hearing this through the cracks in the stone. At least India and Rae did. Nova had run ahead. They were all still in a cave, but a circle of light far ahead was the exit.

"*She* didn't want someone too harsh," Rae mumbled. "She doesn't know how she treated us."

"That was a close one," said India. "It will take them a while to cut through the stone."

"India! Rae!" yelled a voice.

The other two hurried to the cave exit.

Nova was standing open-mouthed. "You have to see this!" she gasped.

CHAPTER 7
HORSE RACE

A whole horse track unfolded across an open space! Jet was frisking about with another horse named Diamond. It was a horse paradise!

The jumping session was at the beginning of the track. There was a low jump, a medium jump, and a high jump, and a line where the galloping session would be. That is where the egg and spoon race would begin. In this race, the rider ran in front of the horse while holding an egg in a spoon.

For some strange reason, there were guards along the exit. Whenever someone got near them, they would challenge him or her to a race.

"India, they're challenging people to races," Rae told her. "If you can make it past one of those guards, we can proceed through the passageway."

"You want me to race that guard?" asked

India.

Rae thought that India felt discouraged, but Nova believed India knew she could easily win. It turned out that Nova was right.

"Listen, I raced against a group of men and only one of them was faster than I. There's no way he'll win against me."

Nova was beginning to wonder if there was anything India couldn't do—besides cracking ice.

India put on her riding helmet and boots and strode up to the guard.

"I challenge you to a race," she said. He seemed surprised that he would be racing a girl.

His horse was a bay stallion that was much larger than the other horses. "This is Evan," he told India.

"That's an interesting name for a horse," India thought. She found Jet and rode him to the starting line. The other guards smirked at Jet. He looked like a midget next to Evan.

The trumpet rang out, and the horses started. First, the guard was in the lead. He made it past the first two jumps, but as soon as he came to the high jump, Evan stopped.

"You can do this, Jet," India told her horse. He braced himself and sailed over the jump.

"Evan! They're ahead of us!" yelled the guard. Still, Evan would not jump; instead, he rode around it and went on to the galloping session.

Even though Evan was bigger, Jet was faster. Jet was now at least eight feet ahead of Evan. The guard was sure that India would win.

Then suddenly he yelled, "Ditch!" Jet wheeled around. He raced back to the starting line.

"No!" yelled India.

"Cheater!" screamed Nova.

India tried to turn him back, but the guard had won the race.

"Luke!" yelled the judge. Luke must have been the guard because the judge was yelling at him furiously.

Then the judge talked to India. "I'm sorry about Luke. It's just that he has never raced a girl before and was upset that you were in the lead.

Come to think of it, no one has ever made it past any of our guards before."

Then India looked sideways at Rae and Nova.

"Come meet my friends, Rae and Nova," India replied. The judge seemed to recognize Nova, and Nova definitely recognized him.

"I know you," she stated. "Aren't you Andrew Milton, the judge from the town horse racing?"

"Yes, I am," he answered. "Call me Andy."

Then a blonde-haired girl who looked about eleven asked with excitement, "Did she make it, Andy? Did she? Did she?"

"That's Lydia," Andy told the girls. "She's my sister."

"Did you win against Luke?" Lydia asked.

"No, I didn't," answered India. "I did get ahead of him though."

"Did you really?" asked Lydia. "You are amazing!" Lydia could hardly speak.

"We'll have to spend the night," India told Andy. "It's getting late."

Andy invited the girls into their large house. Lydia talked to the girls.

"I can't believe you made it past Evan," she marveled. "He's the fastest horse we have."

"Why do the guards challenge everyone to a horse race?" asked Rae.

"Yellaburg wouldn't let this be a free track," she answered.

"Yellaburg?" asked Nova. "That is our home-town – I mean – my home town." She glanced sideways at Rae, who could be from Grystall.

"Let me tell you a secret," said Lydia. "We're horse race judges while above ground, but actually, we're sorcerers. That's how I know all this stuff."

"Good to know," muttered Nova.

"Grystall was threatened by Yellaburg three times," said Lydia. "When we built this track, the town began to threaten us again."

"You mean we're in Florei?" asked Nova.

"Almost," answered Lydia.

THE STORY OF YELLABURG AND GRYSTALL

LONG AGO, IN THE TIME OF SERVENTSA CAROLINA, FLOREI WAS NOT A TOWN YET. (IN GRYSTALL, PEOPLE DON'T SAY, "IN 1765, WE WERE THREATENED BY YELLABURG." INSTEAD, THEY SAY, "IN THE TIME OF SERVENTSA CAROLINA, WE WERE THREATENED BY YELLABURG." IT'S A MUCH LONGER SENTENCE, BUT IT IS A TRADITION WE'VE USED, FROM JENNA TO SHIRLEY).

WHEN CAROLINA'S DAUGHTER, SHIRLEY, WAS BORN, A SPY FROM YELLABURG TOLD CAROLINA THAT IF SHIRLEY WAS TO BE CROWNED, IT WOULD BE IN YELLABURG. OF COURSE, CAROLINA WOULD NOT GIVE HER DAUGHTER TO THIS SPY.

"YOU CANNOT CHANGE THE LAW OF SERVENTSA JENNA," HE TOLD THEM. CAROLINA READ THE LAW OF SERVENTSA JENNA. IT SAID THAT A BABY SERVENTSA WOULD BE GIVEN TO YELLABURG TO BE CROWNED OR ELSE YELLABURG WOULD ATTACK.

Carolina felt sure that Jenna's handwriting had been forged, but she did not say this. Instead, she said, "I will not give you Shirley, but the next Serventsa will be yours."

There was a piece of land that Yellaburg and Grystall had fought over for two years, and Shirley had been ruling for a while. The people of Yellaburg thought she must have had a baby by now.

They finally thought of a way to find out if Shirley was hiding her child. They let Grystall have that piece of land. Maybe it would bring more settlers to Grystall, and then nobody could tell the difference between a common settler and a Yellaburgian spy.

Unfortunately, Grystall didn't accept that piece of land. Shirley Serventsa decided to make its population roughly half

Grystallian but not completely own it.

After Shirley named the piece of land Florei, it became more populated.

The Yellaburgian plan was not turning out as they had hoped, so they attacked and finally, Shirley had no choice.

She carefully wrapped the new baby, Kayla, and gave the bundle to her husband.

She knew that Yellaburg would be expecting Kayla.

CHAPTER 8

STAYING WITH THE MILTONS

"What happened to Kayla?" asked Nova.

"She was taken to Yellaburg," answered Lydia, "although somehow they didn't know that it was Kayla. They only knew that she was from Grystall."

"Why didn't they know she was Serventsa Kayla?" asked Nova.

"I don't know," answered Lydia, "I don't even know who Kayla was."

Neither India nor Nova realized that Rae wasn't talking. She was only thinking about her life and then Kayla's. She thought, "It's possible that *I'm* Kayla."

Then she told herself, "No, that can't be true. If I were Serventsa Kayla, Landei would have said something."

For the first time in her life, Rae tried to hide

her rose medallion. If she was Kayla, she didn't want Lydia to get excited. She had seen how enthusiastic the girl had been around India just because she had overtaken Luke and Evan. Imagine if Lydia knew Rae was Kayla Serventsa.

"You know so much, Lydia," Nova marveled. "I've never studied in my life." Nova immediately regretted her words.

"I can teach you," Andy told her. "You can take these books with you." Andy handed her three black leather bound books. "We'll start at the beginning," he continued as he led her into the study.

"I'll show you the extra bedroom," Lydia told India and Rae.

The extra bedroom was as big as Matthew's room back at Corvate Manor.

"The single bed is for Rae, and the bunk bed is for India and Nova," Lydia said. So now Rae knew that was a bunk bed in the middle of the room.

Just then India came in. She had been lagging behind to look at the trophies won by famous riders. In the extra bedroom, there was picture of a woman riding on the track. Her name was Lily Anne Mabel.

"Who's that?" asked India. India could tell that Lily was a rider. She was very interested in riders.

"That's our founder," answered Lydia. "She didn't ride professionally though. She was not allowed to because she was a woman." The three went back into the living room where Nova was.

Lydia shared everything she learned from Andy. She was having Andy read a book called *The Alphabet Storm* to her. She was also learning her numbers.

"If we're not in Florei, where are we?" asked India.

"We're in Yellaburg," answered Lydia.

She led them into the dining room. "Now we're in Florei.

"You mean we're right on the line?" asked Nova.

"Apparently," answered Lydia. "There wasn't a Florei in the time when Lily built this track, so I guess she didn't notice."

"Have you seen the extra bedroom?" Rae asked Nova. "It's as big as Matthew's room back at Corvate Manor!"

Rae ran upstairs with India and Nova. On the way, she told them about the bunk bed, but then wished she hadn't.

"Who gets the top bunk?" they asked at the same time.

"Here we go again," Rae mumbled.

"I should get the top bunk because I'm – uh – older!" yelled Nova. Rae was surprised. She had seen children say that they should have the larger share of something because they were older, but Nova was twenty-seven.

"Break it up!" Rae shouted. Soon everything was a hullabaloo again. It sounded something like this:

India: "You're acting childish, Nova!"

Nova: "Who are you calling childish?"

Rae: "Not another argument!"

Lydia: "Stop it!"

Andy: "What's going on in here?"

After all of that, they had dinner. Rae had never seen such a grand meal. There was cornbread and chicken and salad. They ate by candlelight. Nova asked for the recipe for the chicken. Andy gave her a card with the recipe. This is what it was:

The best chicken recipe EVER

1. Cook chicken for 20 minutes.

2. Cover with cream sauce.

3. Cook for another 10 minutes.

4. Take out of the oven and serve.

The best cream sauce recipe EVER

1. Mix cream with garden peas.

2. That's basically all there is to it.

Everyone laughed at what Andy wrote for step two of the cream sauce. They were all surprised that the cornbread had yellow cream in it to make it look golden brown. The salad looked even better than the ones Mrs. Corvate had. It was not really a salad, but sliced vegetables on top of a tomato sauce.

The dessert was the best of all. Lydia had her own pear tree above ground. She made the dessert from sliced pears and crushed apricots. Then it was Lydia's bedtime.

"We'd better be getting on to bed, too," India told Andy. She was cross because she had just let Nova have the top bunk.

"I did it to stop the argument," she kept telling Rae.

Nova scrambled up to the top bunk. The blanket was winter-blue, and it had roses on it. India's blanket was white with designs of horses and riders. Rae's blanket was a sort of chart. India helped her read the stitching of words. It looked something like this:

Serventsa Jenna. Population: 534. King: William.

Serventsa Tina. Population: 607. King: William II

Serventsa Abby. Population: 689. King: Edwin

Serventsa Marian. Population: 728. King: Franklin

Serventsa Emily. Population: 837. King: Franklin II

Serventsa Carolina. Population: 856. King: Franklin III

Serventsa Shirley. Population: 901. King: Mark

CHAPTER 9

LADYLIKE

"Rise and shine, girls!" Andy's cheerful voice called.

Rae opened her eyes and found that she could not stretch out her legs. Someone had short-sheeted her bed! Nova screamed. She found herself with a blanket that had horses on it. India found herself with the girly blankets.

"Andy, why did you wake them?" Lydia was standing at the door with string, honey, cream and a fishing pole. "I was planning to prank you."

"What is the meaning of this?" asked Nova.

Nova seemed to be the only one who was angry. Rae was trying to get her legs out of the short sheet, while India was climbing out of her bunk. Lydia showed them her plan. It looked like this:

1. *Short-sheet Rae's bed.*

2. *Switch India and Nova's blankets.*

3. *String the yarn around the room.*

4. *Spread honey on Rae.*

5. *Make Nova a cream hairstyle.*

6. *Swing the monster mask into India's bunk.*

"What is the meaning of this?" asked Nova again.

Suddenly Nova acted like a proper lady, which is what she had learned to do her whole life. "This is a big disgrace! Why, my hair and clothes would have been ruined! I will not live here any longer."

"Nova, what are you talking about?" Rae was trying to get Nova back to her normal self.

"Who are you?" Nova asked, looking at India.

"India Seveta," she answered. "Or was it Sereta?" India could not remember her last name.

"It's a disgrace to not know your last name," Nova answered. Nova looked down at her clothes.

Even though Andy had let the girls borrow extremely clean horse riding outfits, Nova still thought they were not as elegant as they could be. They were not dresses.

"Do you have any calico *dresses*?" asked Nova.

"I'm sorry, Nova," answered Andy. "Lydia doesn't have any calico *or* dresses."

Rae didn't know whether this was Nova or Marilyn. Nova seemed shocked at the thought that Lydia didn't have any dresses.

"Are you sure you're Nova?" asked Rae.

"Of course," she answered. "Who did you think I was, Marilyn? We look nothing alike."

"I guess," Rae thought. She would have said it out loud, but she didn't want to get into any trouble with the new Nova.

"This is a very grand place you have," Nova told Andy. She gasped, "You're Andrew Milton!"

"Call me Andy," he answered.

"I really mustn't. Mother told me to never call gentlemen by their first name, and definitely not by a nickname. So, you're Miss Milton."

"Oh no!" thought Rae. "You can be proper around us, Nova, but please don't be proper with Lydia!"

When Nova walked away into the kitchen with "Mr. Milton" and "Miss Milton," India finally said, "I've got it!"

"What have you got?" asked Rae hoping that India was still the same.

"Nova has been put into a simple trance," she answered.

"How do we break the trance?" asked Rae.

"Nova's mother believed that young ladies could not do the things they do now. To break the trance, we need to act how Nova was taught."

"You mean wear dresses and never go outside?" asked Rae.

"Exactly," answered India.

Being a proper lady was harder than it looked. First, Nova had to give them lessons on what to wear.

"For special occasions, you must try to look prettier than you really are."

"Did that mean wearing frilly clothes?" Rae thought to herself.

"You must wear clothes that make you stand out," said Nova. "You must wear dresses that are in style."

She showed them what "in style" meant. The dresses were pink calico that had ruffles along each side.

Then Nova taught them how to serve tea, "You do not take tea when you want to. You take it when someone gives it to you. When you are serving tea, you wait until the guests have been served first. Now, I want you to try it yourself."

Rae was about to start yelling, but then Nova stopped. She looked around. She seemed surprised that she was actually serving tea.

"What did I miss?" she asked.

"She's out of the trance!" said India.

"What trance?" asked Nova.

Rae and India explained everything that had happened. Once Nova had forgotten about the trance, she could finally focus on studying. She was keeping Andy occupied by asking him to teach her new things. She mastered addition and subtraction that day.

India was often challenging people to horse races and winning all of them, of course. Rae spent time with Lydia. She had plenty of stories to tell Rae including one about a half-spirit, half-human named Cyan.

Finally, the girls had to leave the horse track. Since Andy and Lydia were sorcerers, they had a lot of magical items. They gave the three girls a spare tent, a basket that would refill with food whenever it was empty, and six spices.

"You'll need them," Andy told the girls.

"Goodbye and thank you for letting us stay here," Nova answered.

Now they could talk to each other again.

"I'm glad that trance didn't stay on me forever," Nova told them. "I don't like being a proper lady."

"Neither do I," Rae and India mumbled.

They walked for the rest of the day, sometimes resting in a comfortable spot.

"We should set up the tent," Rae told India.

"What are you looking at me for?" asked India.

"I think you're the only one who knows how to pitch a tent," answered Rae.

That night, Rae was thinking about her friends. She never knew how hard proper life was, and Nova was treated like that all the time. Then she thought about India. She wondered if she liked being the one who did everything because only she knew how. Then again, she didn't seem very happy about pitching the tent without any help. This could only mean one thing. India was jealous.

CHAPTER 10

THE JEALOUSY PLAN

"Jealous?" asked India with disbelief. "I'm not jealous."

"I just thought that because you always…" Rae began.

"Be quiet, Rae!"

"She won't listen," Rae told Nova. "I wish she'd just admit it."

"You can't make her," Nova responded.

Nova sat down with three books. She wrote I AM NOVA on a slate. India sat down with her. India would be Nova's teacher until they got to Florei.

"Write the alphabet on the slate, Nova," India told her.

Nova wrote this: A C B D E F G I H J K M L N O Q P R S T V U W X Z Y

"Nova, 'H' comes before 'I'," said India.

"It does?" asked Nova.

"Yes, and 'P' comes before 'Q'," said India. "We'll discuss everything else later. Now, write – um – 'Rae'."

Nova wrote: R-A-Y

"Nova, it's R-A-E," corrected India.

"How should I know that?" asked Nova.

"Let's move on to arithmetic," said India. "Do you know two times eight?"

"That's easy," responded Nova. "Sixteen!" She had started multiplication yesterday after doing addition and subtraction with Andy.

Both Andy and India were more interested in math than reading, so Nova was slightly ahead in math.

"Good!" said India. "Do you know four times four?"

"Seventeen," answered Nova.

"Close – it's sixteen," India said.

"Then how can two times eight be sixteen if four times four is sixteen?" asked Nova. "There aren't two sixteens, are there?"

"Why don't you just write words starting with the letter 'I'," said India.

India sat down with her math. Nova saw the word "ISOSCELES" in India's math book.

It started with "I", so Nova wrote it down. After a long time, India checked Nova's words. She had written:

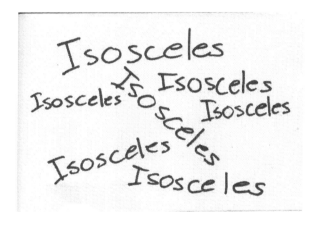

"Isosceles?" asked India. "Do you even know what that means?"

"No, but it starts with 'I'," answered Nova.

"I didn't mean write the same word over and over," groaned India. "You could have written I-N-D-I-A."

"What does that spell?" asked Nova.

"India," answered India.

"That's impossible," said Nova. "If India started with 'I' it would make the 'I' sound, not the sound it makes when saying '*In*dia.'"

"Rae, is there an easier way to help Nova with spelling?" asked India.

"Not that I know of," answered Rae.

"So, is she definitely jealous because we don't have to do as much work?" asked Nova making sure that India couldn't hear her.

"Definitely," answered Rae.

"What did you say?" asked India.

They didn't answer. Nova and Rae went into the tent so India couldn't hear them, and Rae wrote out a plan:

1. India knows more than both of us.

2. India will never admit she's jealous.

3. If we're going to stop India from being jealous, we have to be practical because India knows more than both of us.

"You already said that," said Nova.

4. When it's time to unhitch the tent, I'll do it because it would be very unlikely…

5. …for me to do it.

"You could have just put that in number four," Nova told her.

"Oh, be quiet," said Rae.

6. But India would have to be doing something else so as not to see me unhitching the tent.

7. India will never admit she's jealous.

"You already said that," Nova reminded her.

"Be quiet, Nova. I'm thinking," said Rae.

8. If you were pretending to study very hard things, India might study with you.

9. Then I could unhitch the tent.

10. Without her knowing.

11. Then hopefully she won't be jealous anymore.

"You want me to pretend to study mythology or something?" asked Nova. "I don't even know what the order of the alphabet is."

"I just want you to hold this book," said Rae.

She handed Nova *The Guide to Ancient Script*, "See what you can do with it."

Nova slowly walked towards India. "Oh, hello India," said Nova nervously. "I was just looking at this book."

"You want to learn ancient script already?" asked India.

"Oh right, that," said Nova. "I just wanted to move a step higher."

"You need to learn how to read properly if you're going to learn ancient script," said India.

"Well, you never know what I could do," Nova answered.

"You think you could actually learn ancient script?" asked India.

"If Rae can do it, I can," said Nova.

"She can't," India reminded her.

Rae carefully took a stake out of the ground. It bounded back, but it didn't hit her, so she continued unhitching the tent.

Nova looked at the lowercase page, while India told her what letters they were.

Rae had finished with the tent stakes. She unclipped the tent from the wire until the only remains of the tent were three wires.

"Now the trouble starts," Rae thought. She took the end of the wire and tried to lift it out of the ground. The wire sprung up and hit Rae.

"Ow!" she yelled.

"What's going on?" asked India, who had just noticed Rae.

"I'm – uh – trying to unhitch the tent," answered Rae.

"You don't even know how to unhitch a tent," said India.

"Exactly," answered Nova, hoping that the message had been sent.

"Oh, all right, I was jealous," admitted India.

"Why?" asked Rae, who felt that there was not a right to be jealous for something like that.

"You don't understand." said India. "It's hard to do everything. I just didn't like it when the only reason was because only I knew how."

Rae felt she had to say something. She could have really gotten hurt, "You know, India, you may…"

"I know," interrupted India. "You could have really gotten hurt. I now know that it's dangerous for someone to do something they don't know how to do. I can change that now."

"By the way, India, can I use this book?" asked Nova holding up *The Guide to Ancient Script*.

"Well, doing that certainly isn't dangerous," answered India.

Rae and Nova winked. They walked on until India said they were almost at the orphanage. Rae was very nervous. She was minutes away from learning about her family. They walked on with India in front because only she knew the way.

"Wow, Rae! How did you do that?" asked Nova.

"Oh, you mean what happened with India?" asked Rae.

Nova nodded. "If you could do that with everyone, the whole planet of Calmatza would be a better place."

Rae thought about that, "I could make the world a better place."

CHAPTER 11
A SECRET REVEALED

"We're almost there," India announced as she took the map out of her pocket.

Ψου αρε γεττινγ χλοσερ το Φλορει Ορπηαν αγε. Υντιλ Μρσ. Εδωαρδσ φινδσ ψου, ηιδε ιν τ ηε βροομ χλοσετ. (You are getting closer to Florei Orphanage. Until Mrs. Edwards finds you, hide in the broom closet.)

India could see light ahead. They walked on until they reached the opening and stepped out into the city. It had been a long time since the girls had breathed fresh air and felt the warm sunshine.

"Welcome to Eastern Floreian Orphanage!" said India.

Rae stared at the building in front of her. It was a tall, old-looking building that didn't seem very clean.

"Don't worry, it's a lot better on the inside," said India.

"How can you be sure?" asked Nova. "Things might have changed since you were twelve."

"It's eleven," corrected India.

"Well, whenever it was, it was at least seven years ago," said Rae.

Nova began to ask India questions. "What if Mrs. Edwards doesn't recognize you? What if she doesn't know about Rae? What if she thinks you're just a servant?"

"I'm not a servant," India reminded her.

Nova went on like that for a long time.

"I wonder why the map told us to hide in the broom closet," said Rae. "Do you know where it is?"

"Oh sure, there are many broom closets," said India. "Just try to stay out of Austin's way."

"Who's Austin?" asked Rae.

"He's the son of Mrs. Edwards," answered India. "He teases all the orphans and pretends to be their parents coming to get them."

"He sounds terrible," remarked Nova.

"He is," answered India. "I'd say he's about nineteen now."

"Did he ever tease you?" asked Rae.

"Yes, but I didn't mind," answered India. "I was always stronger than he was."

The girls were at the entrance to the orphanage. Rae felt hot with anxiety. For the first time, she wanted to be a Serventsa. She wanted to be the lost daughter of Shirley Serventsa, or as India called it, Verlinetasem.

"Hey Yankee Doodle Indy!" a loud voice called.

"Austin, you keep quiet!" India yelled.

"Was that Austin?" asked Nova.

"Did he just call you 'Yankee Doodle Indy'?" asked Rae.

"He made up nicknames for everyone in the orphanage," said India. "Timothy was Tiny Timmy, and Charley was…"

She stopped, wondering if she should tell them what Austin called Charley.

"Well?" asked Rae.

"He called him Charlotte," answered India finally.

Nova and Rae looked bewildered.

"He's a boy!" exclaimed Nova. "That is really inappropriate."

"Well, the other boys sure thought it was funny," said India. She opened the big, old-looking doors. Yes, she was right again. The inside did look better. There were bunk beds along the walls and many orphans, some as young as four years old.

Rae could have looked forever, but she knew that she would have to hide in the broom closet just as the map said to.

"There's a broom closet over there," said India. She opened a door that looked like part of the wall, and slid in between the brooms.

Nova and Rae followed her. It was a tight fit, but if they disobeyed the map, then something would go wrong. Rae heard voices from outside. First, a man's voice growled fiercely without saying a word. Another man yelled and dropped a glass. A woman and a girl laughed. A baby cried, two children fought over a doll and finally…

"Knock, knock! Who's in there?" The same woman who had laughed was knocking on the closet door.

"Leave this to me," India whispered.

"It's 9 1 4 4 9 1," India answered.

"9 1 4 4 9 1?" asked Rae. "What's that?"

"That's my name in code," answered India. "Mrs. Edwards loves code. She used to be a spy."

"You can't be," the woman's voice said back. "It's says here that 9 14 4 9 1 left to be a servant for Mrs. Victoria Corvate."

"She did," India stated.

"India?" asked the woman. "Yes, it's me," answered India.

She opened the closet door, and saw Mrs. Edwards' bright face.

"Welcome back, India!" Mrs. Edwards hugged her until India told her what they had come for.

"Kayla Serventsa?" asked Mrs. Edwards. "Well, Shirley did show me the baby, but I expect she's grown up now. I wouldn't recognize her."

Rae didn't know what to say. "Will I have to find out on my own?" she thought.

"Who are these young girls you brought with you?" asked Mrs. Edwards.

"Well, this is Nova and Kayl – I mean Rae," said India.

Mrs. Edwards looked at Rae closely. "That rose!" she marveled. "I've never seen anything like it!"

Rae knew it was too late to hide her medallion. She burned hot inside, and she felt sick in her stomach. Things whirred through her head as if she were not on Calmatza at all. She felt like she was going to pass out.

"Asdafa borontelle carveto!" Mrs. Edwards exclaimed.

"What's she talking about?" asked Nova.

"I don't know," answered India. "She's talking in Floreian. The only things I know how to say in Floreian are, 'yes,' 'no,' 'hello,' and 'good bye.'"

"That's the first time she hasn't known something," Nova thought. She carefully stepped out of the way in case Rae did pass out. India stepped back too and tried not to make any noise.

"What if I'm not a Serventsa?" thought Rae. "What if she doesn't recognize me?" Thoughts raced through Rae's head.

"Letovia alsmaria siaretiroy!" Mrs. Edwards exclaimed.

"Oh – talk all you want," thought Rae. "Just say I'm a Serventsa."

"Nhatingtyers delfreyta semiriyuen esa!" Mrs. Edwards said.

"Just say something!" Rae yelled.

Everyone was shocked at Rae's outburst. Even some of the orphans were staring at Rae.

Mrs. Edwards stared even harder at Rae. After a few minutes, Mrs. Edwards gasped, "I never thought I would come across you again, Kayla Serventsa."

CHAPTER 12

JOURNEY TO THE EIGHT MOUNTAINS

Nova screamed. India looked shocked. Rae stood open-mouthed.

"Am I really Serventsa Kayla?" asked Rae.

"You have come very far," Mrs. Edwards told *Kayla*.

"What do you mean?" Rae asked.

"I mean – figuring out your family," answered Mrs. Edwards. "You must have had to do some pretty clever deducing."

"How well did you know my mother?" asked Rae.

"I knew her well enough to recognize you," answered Mrs. Edwards. "Now it's up to you to find your family."

"Tell me, India," said Rae, "where do they live?"

"On the hill next to Avakta," answered India.

"Where's Avakta?" asked Rae.

"That's the problem," answered India. "No one knows."

"So, I'm not finding my family?" asked Rae.

"You know your family," answered Mrs. Edwards.

Rae didn't know what she meant. She *didn't* know her family.

"What do you mean?" Rae asked.

Mrs. Edwards had disappeared. She had gone to help a baby with her doll.

"Is there a way to get to Avakta?" asked Nova.

India looked at Rae.

"What are you looking at me for?" asked Rae.

"I think you know the way," answered India. She opened a book that was drenched in Grysetsa. She opened it to page 61. It was all about Verlinetasem.

Nova thought that Verlinetasem was a little complicated. Why couldn't they call Verlinetasems "lost legends?"

"The Verlinetasem of any hidden place is destined to find it," said India.

"The Verlinetasem of a what?" asked Nova.

"The Verlinetasem of any hidden place," India repeated slowly.

"What?" asked Nova.

"I think I know what she means," answered Rae. "I think…"

"Farewell Kayla. Live your life well. I hope someone will find you on the hilltop on the outskirts of Avakta. Let someone find her – Serventsa Kayla."

"No!" yelled Rae.

"What is it?" asked Nova.

"I saw my father," answered Rae. "He was leaving me on the outskirts of Avakta."

"The outskirts of Avakta?" asked India. "I thought you were left on a hilltop?"

"I was," answered Rae.

"Do you still know where that hilltop is?" asked India.

"It's on the hill next to Avakta amid the eight mountains in Grystall," answered Rae. She said this very fast.

"What did you say?" asked India.

"I didn't say anything," answered Rae.

"Yes, Rae, you did," answered India. "I just don't really know what. You were talking so fast."

"Didn't you understand her?" Nova asked. "She said Iz in the will vexed to Caracta in the mid of the freight nountains in Grystall."

"I did not," said Rae. "I didn't say anything."

"I think she said the hilltop was on Avakta," answered India. "I don't know where that is though."

"It's one of the eight mountains," answered Rae.

"What?" asked Nova.

"I didn't say anything," said Rae again.

"Do you know what the mountains are?" asked Nova.

"Alveran, Avakta, Sim, Telanemest, Ofortan, Fectaria, Thervan and Laestlan," answered Rae.

"What's that?" asked India.

"What did I say?" asked Rae.

"Say them in order," Nova told Rae.

"Say what in order?" asked Rae.

"The eight mountains," answered Nova.

"I don't know what they are."

"Rae – you just said them," said India.

"I didn't say anything!" said Rae, getting really annoyed with Nova and India. "I have to say that you've been imagining things. I haven't said anything since I saw my father in that image."

"By the way, the eight mountains can be very dangerous," Rae *didn't say*. "You can't escape their dangerous qualities unless you know their secrets, and it's not possible to go around them."

Nova and India didn't answer. They knew from experience that if they answered, Rae would just say that she hadn't said anything. They wanted to avoid that.

"Alveran is a violent volcano that is always active," said Rae. On Telanemest, fire can shoot up anywhere at any time. Ofortan is the highest mountain and has a dangerously high altitude.

Avakta is a jungle with many wild animals. Fectaria is kind of weird. It looks as high as Ofortan, so you might not even think of climbing it, but when you get to the top, it's no bigger than a good-sized mansion.

Thervan is hardly a mountain. Little pieces of it stick up from the water, but it's mostly underwater. Laestlan has amethysts that are full of evil temptation. Once you touch one, you can't get away from it. Sim doesn't seem to be dangerous. It's very windy, but it's not dangerous."

Even though Nova and India were not responding to Rae, it didn't mean they weren't listening.

"A volcano?" asked Nova. "That's always active?"

"That's what Rae…" India stopped. She didn't want to trigger Rae.

"Why are you guys talking about a volcano?" asked Rae.

"Apparently we have to cross a volcano to get to Avakta," answered India.

"Why?" asked Rae.

"Someone told me that Alveran, one of the eight mountains, is a volcano that's always active," said India.

"You mean it's always erupting?" asked Rae.

"Yes, that's what active means," answered India.

"Then how do Florei and Grystall survive?" asked Rae.

"I don't know," answered India. India had come to the conclusion that if she answered questions with "I don't know," Rae would "answer" it quickly.

India had a habit of being bossy. She never really meant to be, but sometimes she uncontrollably started ordering people around like Mrs. Corvate used to do.

"Nova! Hurry up!"

Nova, who had been lagging behind Rae and India, scurried up the street. Or was it the street?

Nobody noticed that they were walking in The Outlands among hills and mountains.

BANG!!!

"What was that?" asked Nova.

"I didn't hear anything," answered India.

"I didn't say anything," Rae answered.

"I don't mean you," Nova told Rae. "I heard a bang."

A growl of thunder came. Or was it thunder?

"I heard it too," Rae whispered.

"Look out guys!" yelled India.

CHAPTER 13

VOLCANO MADNESS

"Alveran!" screamed Nova.

"What?" asked Rae.

"Alveran!" answered India, "The first of the eight mountains."

"People call that a mountain?" asked Rae, unbelievably shocked. "That's more like a lava-spurting giant!"

The girls were far enough from the volcano so that the lava didn't reach them, but it was still very stressful.

BANG!!!

"How are we supposed to get past that mountain?" asked Nova.

"Ask Rae," answered India.

"Are you crazy?" asked Nova. "Rae wouldn't know the answer."

"Keep your head up and run toward the

mountain," yelled Rae. Rae grabbed India and Nova's hands and ran toward the volcano, which was erupting wildly.

"Rae, how can you suggest that?" asked Nova. "We'll be burned!"

"Just stay with me!" Rae yelled. "I know what to do!"

India suddenly got splashed with the lava!

"It's just ruby Grysetsa!" she exclaimed.

"Grysetsa?" asked Rae. "How can a volcano erupt Grysetsa?"

"I don't know," answered India. "It just does."

"Wait! It's Grysetsa," thought Rae. "Landei!" she yelled.

Landei rose out of the "volcano" crater. The spirit was looking a lot clearer than when Rae last encountered her.

"Kayla, I know this is a shock to you, but you must know that this is my territory."

"Call me Rae," Rae told Landei.

"I own the eight mountains," Landei told them. "I know how to defend against their dangerous qualities."

"How do we get past them?" asked Nova.

"Take this." Landei handed Rae a stick and gave Nova and India cylinder tanks.

India shook the tank vigorously. It was obviously Grysetsa because it didn't slosh around, and Grysetsa doesn't move when shaken.

"Landei, what are we supposed to do with these?" asked Rae, but Landei had disappeared.

"By the way," Landei told them. The spirit's voice came out of the crater. "It's not Grysetsa on the other side of the volcano. It's real lava."

"How do we get past that?" asked India.

"Use the wand," answered Landei, "Its name is Sorvara."

Rae was tempted to say, "You mean the stick?" but she knew that would not help anything.

"Just point it at a lava geyser, and close your eyes," the voice told Rae. "When the wand starts to turn pale, recharge it with the Grysetsa tubes.

Rae didn't know what Landei was talking about, but she decided to do what the spirit said. The three girls walked to the other side of the mountain. After hiking for a while, the girls approached the side with spurting lava. All the girls could see were deep crevasses in the mountain.

Somehow, Rae knew there was lava coming from one of the crevasses. She raised her arm and pointed at a hole in the mountain. She closed her eyes. A sort of energy flowed through her.

The lava spurted out, but no sooner had the energy of Rae's wand hit it, the lava became solid rock that plugged up the crevasse.

"Rae, you can stop now," India told her. Rae opened her eyes. She saw the towering stone shape.

"Take it with you," Landei's voice told Rae.

"We have to take it with us," Rae told the other two.

"You mean – take that stone?" asked India.

"I guess," answered Rae.

"It's huge!" yelled Nova, "It probably weighs a ton!"

"Landei told me to," said Rae.

"I guess we should trust Landei," Nova told

India.

"Come on," Rae urged them.

Nova and India tried to lift the stone, while Rae summoned Landei. She yelled into the sky, "Landei! We can't lift the stone!"

The spirit did not answer.

"Landei!" Rae yelled again, louder this time.

Landei didn't answer. Instead, the spirit simply appeared in the sky. She was silent for a while. Finally, she told Rae, "Load it on Jet."

"Where's Jet?" asked India. "Rae! Nova! We forgot Jet! We must have left him at Andy and Lydia's house!"

"Landei, where's Jet?" asked India.

"He is not far from you," Landei answered. "He is riding through the woods with two good friends of yours," Landei told her. "Besides, I don't mean Jet your horse; I mean the Jet Glider."

"What's that?" asked India.

Landei didn't have to answer. It was already flying through the air just above her. The Jet Glider was a black, bamboo, dragon-like glider that sailed through the air just like a dragon. It landed very close to the plugged hole.

Landei reappeared. "The Jet Glider can stand enormous friction and high altitude; it can sustain a temperature of over 1000 degrees and can lift very heavy objects from place to place," she said. Landei demonstrated this by pulling a lever.

The "wing" of the Jet Glider pulled the large stone into its black bamboo compartment in the back. Even though it was bamboo, the Jet Glider could easily carry the stone. It was amazing. Before Rae could say anything, the Jet Glider whisked off.

Landei had disappeared into the Grysetsa. The three girls were soaked in red Grysetsa, but they didn't seem to notice. Rae strode on through the volcano feeling very calm and brave. India was not as calm, but she could walk alongside Rae without feeling too anxious.

Usually, Nova would be nervous if she was walking through a volcano with two girls younger than her, but she trusted Rae to not let them burn.

Another spurt of lava came out of a hole that was much bigger than the last one. Rae stopped it easily. Suddenly, she knew that this was an extraordinary power. Even doing just what Landei had told her, she seemed to have known all along what to do.

The Jet Glider flew above the three girls and landed in front of the towering stone.

India looked at the Glider. "Which lever did she pull?" she asked.

Rae pulled the lever nearest to her without thinking. It was a red lever and did not look like it was connected to anything that would make the wing pick up the large, grey stone that was much larger than the last stone. Surprisingly, it worked. The wing easily picked up the stone and placed it in the compartment.

Rae did the same thing with the next crevasse and the next. The wand was a pale grey after the last two holes.

"How do you recharge this thing?" asked Rae.

India discovered two wires. She connected the wire on her bottle to Nova's, and connected the wires onto Rae's wand. The wand charged up quickly and automatically.

Rae discovered that after every four crevasses, the wand had to be recharged. After all the holes were plugged with stone, the three girls realized they were soaked, but they didn't mind.

That evening, they dried off in the tent. When India said she was pretty sure the next mountain was Telanemest, Rae wasn't worried.

"Surely the next mountain couldn't be worse," she thought. But it *was* worse.

CHAPTER 14

ADVENTURES OF FIRE

"Is that Telanemest?" asked Nova. "That just looks like a ball of flames!"

"How are we supposed to get over that?" asked Rae.

"Use the stones and spices," Landei's voice rang out.

"*What* stones and *what* spices?" asked Nova.

"The stones you transformed from lava, and the spices the Miltons gave you," answered Landei.

Rae still had those spices. She took out oregano, basil, cinnamon, cloves, nutmeg and black pepper. The Jet Glider landed in front of the girls again.

"Throw the stones," Landei instructed them.

India and Rae pulled a blue lever of The Jet Glider and a catapult threw the stones toward the mountain. The flames separated, making a walkway. They walked it for about an hour until they came to all the rocks they had thrown. Telanemest was not as wide as Alveran, so the six large stones they had thrown were in the way of their path.

"Now what?" asked Nova.

"I think we'll have to climb them," Rae answered.

Nova felt scared. Mountains were one thing, very jagged stones surrounded by fire were something else. India carefully climbed up and around the highest stones. Rae went up after her, leaving Nova to follow. She silently ascended.

Once the three girls got to the last of the stones, India told Rae to hand Nova the oregano and basil. Rae threw the oregano and basil toward her. Nova caught the oregano, but the basil went all over the place. Most of the contents were gone, but there was enough to do what India was planning. Rae had the cinnamon and cloves and threw to India the nutmeg and pepper.

"Now shake the first spice!" India demanded.

"I don't know what the first spice is!" Nova yelled back.

"In your case, it's the basil," answered India. "Rae, yours is the cloves."

India shook her black pepper along with a mixture of basil where it had spilled everywhere. The three spices joined together and made a greenish-blackish mixture. A wall of fire appeared in front of them.

"Throw your other spices!" India yelled. Quite literally, India threw her nutmeg and started climbing down her rock and running down the walkway toward the flames. Rae and Nova followed her, throwing their spices. As soon as the spices hit the fire, they separated into many little laser beams.

India had no trouble at all with getting through the beams. She just slid under one and jumped over a few others until she was on the other side. Rae and Nova shrugged. Rae ducked underneath the highest beam. Nova followed her, not paying any attention to the beam in front of her.

"Watch out!" yelled Rae.

Nova barely missed the beam. There were no more beams high above, so they could stand up.

"Whoa!" Nova yelled. She barely missed a beam that was dangerously close to her foot.

Rae was ahead of her now and very close to the end.

"Rae – your hand!" yelled Nova. Rae's hand was about to touch a beam.

After a while, both of them had passed all the laser beams. Rae looked very tired, and Nova was about to fall over, but they had come a long way.

"The fireballs are next," India told Rae.

"What fireballs?" asked Rae.

India didn't have to answer.

Fireballs were balls of blazing orange fire that were clearly hotter than normal fire. Rae could feel it.

"How are we supposed to get passed those balls?" asked Nova.

A voice inside Rae's head told her to use Sorvara. Rae pointed it at an extra large ball and closed her eyes. The energy flowed through her again.

"Rae! Watch out!" yelled Nova.

The fire did not stop. The wand had only made the ball change from orange to blue. Rae didn't hear Nova. The ball of blue fire went right through her!

"Nova! India!" she yelled. "This is the blue fire that I felt at the cave!"

"Does it feel like anything?" asked Nova.

"It's not burning, anyway," answered Rae.

"Is that all?" asked India.

"No," answered Rae. "When the fire hit me, I saw my mother."

"Your mother?" asked Nova. "How could you; you don't even know what she looks like."

"I don't know," answered Rae.

"Watch out for those fireballs coming at you!" India yelled.

Rae pointed the wand at two fireballs. The blue balls of flame went right through Nova and India.

"What did you see?" asked Rae.

"I saw Marilyn playing with me outside," Nova told Rae.

"I saw myself in a professional horse race," India told Rae.

The three girls walked on. Fireballs came and went. The second time India had seen her mother, whom she had never known, she looked familiar somehow. Nova had seen her mother and sister climbing trees and wearing leggings. Even though Rae had been through many balls of fire, she always saw her mother.

Very soon Sorvara became pale. "It's time for a recharge!" Rae told India.

Sometimes, the wand took a long time to charge, and sometimes it didn't. Rae had to wait nearly an hour once. Her shortest amount of time to recharge was three minutes. Even then, it seemed like a long time.

The three girls were glad to get some rest after the big day. India barely had enough energy to set up the tent.

Nova didn't know what Ofortan would be like. If it had a dangerously high altitude, there was no way that the wand would do them any good. Nova happened to be the only one thinking about Ofortan. India and Rae were discussing the temperature of normal fire. The blue fire was usually hottest. They weren't thinking about Ofortan.

CHAPTER 15

RIDE ON THE JET

"We're never going to make it up there," Rae told India.

"Even if we do make it to the top, we wouldn't survive for long," India replied.

Nova didn't say anything. She was thinking about what Landei had said about the Jet Glider. The more she thought about it, the more she thought, "Is it possible?"

"Nova, what would you do?" asked India.

"That's it!" Nova exclaimed.

"What?" asked India.

"We could ride the Jet Glider!" answered Nova excitedly.

"The Jet Glider?" asked Rae.

"Weren't you listening?" Nova asked. "Landei said the Jet Glider could stand high altitude."

"Do you know how to drive that thing?" asked

Rae.

"Well, no." answered Nova. "We can manage, though."

The Jet Glider had landed in front of them. India squeezed into the tight cockpit.

"This isn't going to work," Nova told India, who would be driving the Glider.

"It was your idea," India reminded her.

Rae was the lookout. If there was anything in the way, she was supposed to tell India to go a certain direction. Nova was "Jet leader." India was "Jet one," and Rae was "Jet two."

"How do we start this thing?" asked Jet one.

"Wait a minute! I found a book of instructions," Jet leader told Jet one.

"I'll read it!" Jet two called from the back of the Glider. "Pull the blue rope!"

"Which one?" asked Jet one.

"It says the one behind the minuscule hammer!" Jet two called back.

India looked at the two blue ropes carefully. One of them was behind a little red button and one of them was in front of a little lever that India knew was called a hammer.

India called back to Rae, "I found the right rope, but it's in front of the miniscule hammer, not behind it."

"Just pull it and see what happens," Jet leader told Jet one.

India quite literally pulled the rope. It came off in her hands. The Jet started to shake.

"It's ready to fly!" Jet leader told Jet two.

But it wasn't. It jerked violently, and remained on the ground. Jet one finally managed to get the Glider in the air. It sped off in various directions at first, but India eventually figured out which blue rope to pull. It happened to be the little dark blue one that hung on the ceiling behind the little levers on a grey panel. India had accidentally pulled the escape rope that would take them anywhere that was safe. Since there wasn't any danger, the Jet didn't know which way to take them.

India was in a very cramped position in the cockpit of the Jet Glider. She could hardly pull the rope without bumping her head on the ceiling. She finally managed to reach up in the little space she had and jerk the rope. Now the Glider was in the air.

"Pull the miniscule hammer!" Jet two called to Jet one.

As soon as India pulled the miniscule hammer, Nova commanded Rae to adjust the wing angle.

"Pull the left wing to a right angle!" Jet leader shouted.

Rae pulled the left lever until the wing was at a right angle to Ofortan. They were still at low altitude and the air was breathable.

Even though Nova had no idea what she was yelling, she enjoyed giving commands in the cargo Glider.

"Vestale 3, Vestale 7, 1000 redgar, 789 redgar!" Rae called to the front of the Glider.

The settings on the speed monitor clock looked something like a speedometer. This is what they looked like:

Vestale 1   Vestale 7

                             Vestale 3

Redgar 3000   Redgar 2000

                   Redgar 789

"Vestale 3, Vestale 1, 7OQ!" Jet two yelled.

"7OQ?" asked Jet one.

"Press the red button!" yelled Rae.

"Rae, did you hear me?" asked Nova, "Right wing neutral!"

Rae pulled the right lever until it was neutral with the browner looking mountain.

India pressed the button that read **7OQ** on it.

The Jet took a sharp turn upward. Rae fell backward and Nova landed on top of her. India pressed a blue button that read "*Altitude Shield*." She had no idea what an altitude shield was, but she knew the Glider was getting to a very high altitude.

A metal coating covered the bamboo body of the Glider. It was obviously the altitude shield.

The Glider was still going up. It was climbing a side of Ofortan.

"Ready – now shift!" Rae yelled to the front.

India pressed a button that read "*Release.*" The Glider went sharply downward toward the ground. It looked like the Glider was going to crash. India controlled the Glider until it landed safely on the ground in front of Ofortan's base.

Rae and Nova opened the door of the Glider. India got out first because she was desperate to leave her cramped position in the Glider.

"I'm glad to get out of there," gasped India.

"Well, at least you weren't thrown around all over the front of the Glider," said Rae.

Nova thought about what she had done. She had managed to pilot a Glider. She and India talked about the adventure. India had never driven a Glider before. She was surprised they had landed safely.

Rae found three talking devices inside the Glider. They allowed people to talk from faraway places. India thought they might be useful. Rae had no idea what the next mountain would be, but she was sure that it would be very odd.

That evening, she settled into the tent with Nova and India. The next morning, they arrived at Fectaria. It was unusual, but Rae seemed to be the only one who knew what to do. After all, Fectaria was no ordinary mountain. It never was, and it never would be.

CHAPTER 16

THIS WAY! NO THAT WAY!

"Is that Fectaria?" asked Nova. "Rae was right. It's almost as high as Ofortan."

"It's really as big as a good-sized mansion," India reminded her.

"What size is that?" asked Nova.

"About the size of Mrs. Corvate's, Rae *didn't say*."

India and Nova were lost in thought while Rae started putting together her big plan. Rae knew that Fectaria was not as high as it looked by listening to Nova and India, and she had a vision of what Fectaria might look like at its true height.

"Do you know how to lasso?" asked Rae.

"Yes," answered India. "Why?"

"If you could lasso this rope then we might be able to find out Fectaria's true height," answered

Rae.

India took the rope Rae was holding. It had a peg tied to one end. India spun the rope over her head again and again. She twirled it so high that it looked like she was about to spin away with it. Finally, she let go of one end. The peg stopped at about a quarter of the way up Fectaria.

"Well, that's a start," Rae told India. "We don't really know if that's the true height."

"Ow! You stepped on my foot!" yelled India.

"Sorry! I can't see you!" yelled Nova.

Rae, Nova and India had started climbing Fectaria.

"This was a bad idea," Nova told Rae. Or what she thought was Rae.

The girls had made themselves invisible so they could see well. India had told Rae and Nova that invisibility powder helped people see invisible things. It did help them see well. India saw colors she had never seen before, like ultraviolet and infrared. Nova saw a tiny, microscopic bug, and Rae even saw Fectaria's true height.

"A little bit to the right!" Rae yelled behind her.

It turned out that India and Nova were 20 feet in front of her and were going to the left. Rae didn't know that and assumed they were following her to the right.

Rae was about half way up Fectaria's true height when she called, "Nova, India are you with me so far?"

Of course Nova and India were separated from Rae, so they didn't answer.

"Nova! India!" she called again. They didn't answer.

"Where are you?!" Rae called, this time into her talking device.

"We're over here on the left side," they answered. "Nova's got the rope I lassoed."

"What are you doing over there?" asked Rae. "That's not the way up; come over here."

"Where are you?" asked India, or rather India's voice.

"I'm on the right side," Rae answered.

"What's the right side?" asked India.

"Seriously, India, can't you tell direction?" asked Rae.

"Of course I can tell direction," she answered. "What do you think I am?"

"Invisible," answered Nova.

"Be quiet!" Rae heard India say through the talking device.

"Well, if you can tell direction then you would know that right is the opposite of left," said Rae.

"Oh," India understood now what Rae wanted them to do.

"Walk to the right," Rae directed.

Nova knew how to tell direction, but she sometimes got confused. Nova went to the left.

"Come on, Nova," India yelled behind her. She walked on without Nova.

"Where are you?" asked India.

She bumped into Rae just then.

"Come on Nova!" India yelled behind her, "Nova?" asked India. "Oh great," she groaned.

"Now we're separated from Nova," she told Rae.

"I think I know where Nova is," Rae reassured

her. "Does she still have that rope that you lassoed to the "top" of the mountain?"

"I think so," answered India.

"That rope isn't invisible," said Rae. "If we can see that rope, then we know Nova can't be far."

The rope was nowhere in sight.

"We'll have to walk until we find it," said Rae.

India and Rae walked until the long rope appeared in sight. It was tense but moving around. Apparently, Nova was holding onto it as if her life depended on it.

"Nova!" India called. "I know you're over here."

"Come toward the rope," Nova's voice told them.

"Actually, you should follow us," Rae told her. "You're going the wrong way."

"How do you know?" asked Nova.

"I can see Fectaria's true height," Rae answered. "We're not far from the top."

"Where are you?" asked Nova.

"Let go of the rope," Rae directed.

"I can't." Nova sounded desperate. "If I let go, I'll fall."

Rae could now see where Nova was. There was a ledge that looked like a porch without rails. In front of it was an almost straight up and down wall. Nova was climbing it.

"Get back onto the ledge!" said Rae.

Nova climbed down the wall and told Rae when she was on the ledge by letting go of the rope. Rae grabbed onto it.

"India do you have another rope?" she asked.

"Of course I do," answered India. "What do you think I am?"

"I think you're ignoring me when I'm trying to hold onto Fectaria with my life!" Nova yelled.

"India!" Rae yelled.

India climbed to the top and threw the rope down to Nova. Nova caught it and hung on very tightly. India drove the peg into the mountain. Nova slowly followed Rae the right way up.

"India, you can shave off the invisibility now," said Rae.

India took a pumping bag and pumped all of the powder off of Rae and Nova and then pumped herself. They looked at each other. They were covered in scratches. They looked up. The false Fectaria was towering above them. The three girls walked down the real Fectaria. When they looked up, they saw a mountain almost as tall as Ofortan.

Rae thought about the invisible adventure. She had seen a mountain that was not as high as it looked. She had figured out its true height. She thought to herself, "That is the true power of a Serventsa."

Nova was talking to her. "How did you do that?" she asked. "How come I didn't see Fectaria's true height?"

Nova told Rae she had been following a microscopic bug. She pronounced it "micosopic."

As India was setting up the tent that evening, she wondered what mountain would be next. Avakta, Thervan or Laestlan?

The next morning, when she got to the mountain, she understood what Rae meant by amethysts.

Laestlan's amethysts were even more beautiful than normal ones. She thought about what they had done to escape the other mountains, and she realized what she had to do. Laestlan could not be escaped by magic.

CHAPTER 17

LAESTLAN: THE AMETHYST PALACE

"Those amethysts are beautiful," Nova gasped.

"Don't be fooled," India reminded her.

"What do you mean?" asked Rae.

"The amethysts are full of evil temptation," answered India. "If you touch one, you will not leave the mountain."

"How are we going to get up there without touching the amethysts?" asked Nova, looking at India.

India was thinking hard. She knew Laestlan could not be escaped by magic.

"Rae, climb up the mountain," India directed.

"We don't know how to escape the powers of this mountain," said Rae.

"Just do it," said India.

Rae uneasily walked up the flat part of Laestlan that was covered in amethysts, and she started to climb the small uphill slope, dodging every one.

"I guess that's how you escape the mountain," India told her.

"*That's* how you get up?" asked Rae in disbelief.

"I figured out that Laestlan cannot be escaped by magic," India told her. "We have to be careful."

"You mean we just have to dodge every amethyst?" asked Nova.

"I guess," India answered. "There's just no way of escaping it magically."

"All right, but be careful," Nova told India.

"Nova, India's done this a million times," Rae reminded her.

"Let's go," said India and climbed up to where Rae was.

Nova followed, thinking that if they escaped Alveran using Rae's wand, and they escaped

Telanemest with spices and stone, and they escaped Ofortan with the Jet Glider…

"Come on, Nova!" India yelled.

Nova followed India, who was already a good distance ahead of her. Rae was glad the mountain was pretty flat or they would never make it. Rae lifted her arms and legs and did everything she had to do to dodge the amethysts.

Nova had never done anything like this before, and for some reason, it seemed harder than when she had to dodge the flames. She thought that staying on a mountain for the rest of her life somehow sounded worse than being burned. She knew that it wasn't worse. If you stayed on a mountain forever, someone was bound to see you and cure you, but if you got burned...

"Hurry up, Nova!" yelled India. "That's the second time!"

The three girls continued to very carefully dodge amethysts. India began to wobble! She quickly caught herself just before she fell on millions of amethysts. "This has got to be the worst mountain there is!" said India.

"Really?" asked Rae. "I still think it was Fectaria."

"I think it was Alveran," said Nova.

"Alveran!" India and Rae exclaimed together.

"Well, you can't blame me for having an opinion!" said Nova.

"Well, according to me, Ofortan was the least terrible," said Rae.

"Not according to me," said India. "How would you like to be squished into a tight cockpit?"

"I think Sim will be the least dangerous," said Nova.

"Nova, we haven't been to Sim yet," said India.

"But Rae only said it was windy," said Nova.

"When did I say that?" asked Rae.

"Nova!" groaned India.

"There is an amethyst palace on this mountain," Rae *didn't say*.

India didn't say anything but Nova said, "An amethyst palace?"

"What amethyst palace?" asked Rae.

"That one," answered India.

Right above them was a gleaming amethyst palace. The jeweled turrets of the palace were so tempting that even India was walking towards them.

"Stop!" said a voice.

The girls looked up. It was Landei. "The amethyst palace has the most amethysts on the entire mountain," she said. "You'll have to be careful not to touch any of them. If you come across a fork in the path, always take the path with a spirit on it."

The three girls nodded. Rae walked into the palace first, then Nova, then India.

They walked for nearly an hour, dodging every amethyst.

"A fork," said Nova.

The other two girls went toward the path with the amethyst on it.

"No!" said Nova. She tried to drag them away to the other path, but her efforts were useless. She was about to give up when she saw a spirit coming towards her.

The bright green spirit helped turn Rae toward the other path, but India kept on walking.

"Stop India!" yelled Nova.

The spirit did not stop India though. Very soon, she melted into the amethyst wall!!

"Why didn't you stop her?" yelled Nova.

"I chose to save Rae," answered the spirit. "India has been melted into the wall."

"What does that mean?" asked Nova indignantly. She was getting impatient with the spirit.

"It means she cannot be saved," answered the spirit. "If she meets us on the other side, she will be lucky, but only one other person has done that."

"Who is that other person?" asked Nova.

"The King," answered the spirit. "He was carrying a baby girl down to Grystall when he got trapped in the wall. I chose to save the baby."

"What happened after that?" asked Nova, sitting down.

Rae had been listening too, and she also sat down to hear the story.

THE SPIRIT'S STORY

LONG AGO, IN THE TIME OF SERVENTSA JENNA, THIS AMETHYST PALACE WAS BORN. EVERYONE LOVED IT AND CAME TO SEE IT, UNTIL MEIANRUS, THE SPIRIT OF EVIL, CURSED IT.

MANY YEARS PASSED, AND NOBODY CAME TO THE PALACE ANYMORE.

I WAS PLACED AT THE FORK TO HELP PEOPLE IF THEY DID COME. ONLY ONE PERSON DID, THOUGH.

THE KING, MARK, WAS CARRYING A LITTLE BABY GIRL WITH HIM. THE AMETHYST TEMPTED HIM, AND I GRABBED THE BABY AWAY FROM HIM.

HE MELTED INTO THE WALL, AND THERE WAS I WITH THE LITTLE BABY. I RAN THROUGH TO THE OTHER PATH, AND I FOUND HIM STANDING THERE.

I REMEMBERED SEEING THE KING SEVEN YEARS EARLIER ON SIM, AND I ASKED HIM WHAT HE'D BEEN DOING. HE

TOLD ME THAT HE HAD BEEN GIVING A BABY GIRL TO YELLABURG. THE BLOOD GLIDER WOULD PICK HER UP. THEN HE TOLD ME ABOUT THE BABY HE WAS HOLDING NOW. SHE WOULD LIVE IN FLOREI, WHICH WAS SAFE FROM YELLABURGIANS. THERE, THE KING WOULD TAKE CARE OF HER AND EDUCATE HER WELL. THEY WOULD LIVE CLOSE TO HIS SISTER-IN-LAW.

WHEN HE GOT THERE AND REALIZED THAT HIS SISTER-IN-LAW'S DAUGHTERS HAD BEEN SENT AWAY, HE DECIDED NOT TO LIVE CLOSE TO HER AT ALL. INSTEAD, HE CHOSE A PLACE NEAR THE FLOREI-GRYSTALL BORDER, WHERE HE, UNFORTUNATELY, GOT SICK AND DIED. HE HOPED HIS DAUGHTER WOULD CONTINUE THE PATH OF LIFE FOR HIS FAMILY.

"So anyway," said the spirit. "I'm not sure she'll make it through."

"Hey!" said a voice. "What's going on here?" India entered the room. "What did I miss?"

Rae and Nova were very glad to see India. They asked her many questions.

"Well, it was like a million little sparks were hitting me, and suddenly I was out of the wall," said India.

"Do you still think Alveran is the worst mountain?" Rae asked.

"No way!" answered Nova. "This mountain was much worse."

Nova and Rae told the spirit's story to India.

India said, "So Shirley Serventsa did have another child."

"I wonder who it is," said Nova.

"Do you think she is still in Florei?" asked Rae.

"I doubt it," answered India. "She's probably off somewhere in The Outlands."

"The story sounds vaguely familiar to me," said Rae.

The girls were so used to dodging amethysts that they didn't have to think about it anymore.

"So, do you think that Thervan's next?" asked India. She was setting up the tent for the night.

"Maybe," answered Nova. "It could be Avakta, or even Sim."

"Well, whatever the next mountain will be, it can't be any worse than this," said India.

"I think the next mountain might be a little bit worse," thought Rae.

CHAPTER 18

THERVAN: THE FLOATING MOUNTAIN

Rae was right. When the three girls arrived at Thervan, the first thing they saw was a huge, rough body of water.

"How are we going to get to the mountain?" asked Nova.

"We'll have to build a boat or something," answered Rae.

Rae looked at India, but India was looking at the mountain. Suddenly, India plunged into the water and stayed there for a few seconds.

Then she popped up and said, "It's a floating mountain!"

"What does that mean?" asked Nova.

"It means that the mountain is floating on the water," answered India, as if it were kind of obvious.

"I know," said Nova, "But how does it help us?"

"Don't you see?" asked India. "We can just swim under it."

India thought that her idea was quite brilliant, but Rae and Nova didn't think so.

"India," said Rae. "Aren't you forgetting something?"

"Oh," said India, "You don't know how to swim, do you?"

"No, we don't," answered Nova.

India thought for a moment and then said, "Well, there goes that plan! Come on, let's go build a boat."

"Wait!" said Rae, "Can't you teach us how to swim?"

"Trust me, Rae," said India, "I can't."

"Sure you can," said Nova. "All you have to do is teach us the basics."

"I know," said India, "but I'm a horrible teacher."

"India," said Rae. "Imagine a Serventsa was telling you to teach us how to swim. What would you do?"

"I would do it, of course," said India. "But there's no Serventsa forcing me to…"

"Yes, India, there is," Rae interrupted. She pointed to herself to emphasize what she had just said.

"All right," said India, "but remember what I said."

Rae and Nova were more determined then ever to go through with this.

"This is Sinxa weed," said India. "It lets you breathe and talk underwater. You only need a few stalks, but I'm just warning you, it tastes…"

"Ugh!" exclaimed Nova, spitting the Sinxa weed on the ground. "How can you eat this?"

"…Horrible," finished India.

"This is disgusting!" said Rae. "Is it really worth being able to breathe and talk underwater?"

"It will be," answered India, "when we have to swim under the mountain."

She led them to the water. "Get in," she said.

Rae got in the water, but Nova held back. "No way!" she said. "I'll get wet if I go in there!"

"That's what's going to happen," said India.

Nova very slowly went in the water.

"Oh, I almost forgot," said India. She went to the bottom, and found two bunches of some reddish thing.

"What's that?" asked Rae.

"It's Evenherla," answered India. "It's the mother of Sinxa weed. When it goes in the water it will turn white. When it starts to turn red again, you'll know when the Sinxa weed is wearing off." She tied a bracelet of Evenherla around their wrists.

"Put your head in the water," India instructed.

They put their heads in the water. Nova took deep breaths full of water. Then she popped her head up. "That felt great," she said.

"Now for the swimming," said India.

She carefully went through the basics of swimming. She had them go out into the deep water and practice keeping their head above water.

"How much longer?" complained Nova, whose arms and legs were aching from treading water.

"Thirty more seconds," answered India.

"Seriously?" said Rae. "I don't think I can do another thirty seconds of this."

"Try to distract yourself," said India. "You'll feel better."

"Easy for you to say," said Nova. "You've been doing this your whole life.

Finally, the thirty seconds were over.

"This was a waste of time," said Rae. "We won't have to keep our heads above water, anyway."

"I was trying to strengthen your arms and legs," said India. "That's the only reason I did that."

She placed two sticks in the ground that were tall enough to stick out of the water. The next thing she had them do was swim from one stick to the other. They both accomplished it, but when India moved the sticks farther apart, Nova gave up altogether.

"I can't do this," she said.

"Well, I guess you'll never be able to swim that far," said India, pointing to the mountain.

"That's how far we have to swim?" asked Nova. She seemed a bit discouraged.

"We have to go under the mountain," said India. "There's probably water on the other side too."

Nova quickly plunged into the water and started for the sticks.

By lunchtime, the lessons were over. The girls ate a quick lunch and started for the water.

They swam faster and harder then they ever had before. They even separated a few times, but once they got to the mountain, they joined together again. They all popped up at the mountain.

"We only have to go to that bank," said India. The bank was actually quite far away.

Nova looked really tired. "Can we rest first?" she asked.

"Alright," said India. "But we're starting after thirty minutes."

When the girls set off again, India, of course,

was completely fine. She loved swimming and didn't want to stop. Nova was only swimming fast because she wanted to get to the bank as quickly as possible.

Rae was well behind the other two, but she was keeping up all right. She began to pull her arms in front of her to move herself forward. She absent-mindedly noticed the Evenherla wristband she was wearing. India and Nova heard a scream behind them. They rushed back toward Rae.

"The Evenherla!" she yelled. "It's turning red! We have to…"

Rae tried to finish the sentence, but it came out in a stream of bubbles! The Sinxa weed was wearing off! The three girls swam up to the surface as quickly as they could. Their heads popped up in the middle of the water. The bank was still a good distance away. For once, Nova was glad that she had done the treading water drill or else she wouldn't have been able to hold herself up.

"There's still more to swim," said Rae. "How are we going to make it?"

"Well, you're in luck," said India. "You're with the most prepared girl in the world."

She handed two pieces of Sinxa weed to the other two. She popped some in to her mouth. The three girls swam the rest of the way without any more interruptions.

"Good," said India. "Now we only have Sim left, and there's no way that can be dangerous!"

"I'm just glad that the swimming is over," said Nova. That evening, she collapsed into the tent even though it was nowhere close to nighttime. They didn't know they were forgetting a mountain.

CHAPTER 19

AVAKTA AND THE EXTRAORDINARY FIVE

Rae and India did not notice Avakta, but Nova did. She tried to remind India and Rae, but they were just talking about swimming.

Just then, Rae screamed. A big, rock statue of an old man was kneeling in front of them. In front of it was Avakta.

"I forgot about Avakta," said India.

"Me too," said Rae. "I didn't expect this creepy man to be here."

"He's made of ore," said India. "He's not real!"

"He's still creepy," said Rae.

"I know how he got there," said India.

"Of course she does," Nova muttered under her breath.

THE ORE ROBBER

LONG AGO, AVAKTA USED TO BE A DESERT. A ROBBER LIVED THERE, AND HE WANTED THE WHOLE WORLD TO HIMSELF.

HE DUG UP ALL THE JEWELS AND STONES IN THE MOUNTAIN AND TOOK THEM TO FLOREI.

THE JEWELS THAT REMAINED GOT ANGRY WITH THE ROBBER AND TURNED THE ENTIRE MOUNTAIN INTO BRICK SO HE COULD NOT DIG ANYMORE.

YEARS PASSED, AND THE ROBBER RETURNED TO AVAKTA AS AN OLD BEGGAR. HE PRAYED TO DEIEVEDE, THE QUEEN OF THE SPIRITS, WITH ORE AS HIS OFFERING.

DEIEVEDE WAS ABOUT TO TAKE PITY ON HIM BUT REMEMBERING WHAT HE'D DONE IN HIS YOUNGER LIFE, TURNED AVAKTA INTO A JUNGLE AND HIM INTO ORE.

IF YOU COME TO AVAKTA, YOU CAN STILL SEE HIS KNEELING FORM.

"It's a chapter from a book," said India.

"What book?" asked Nova, *The Guide to Weird Stories* or something?"

"No!" said India. "It's called, *The Guide to the Eight Mountains*. I have it with me."

"Wait," said Rae. "You've had that book with you the whole time?"

Nova knew what Rae meant.

"You mean that we spent all this time trying to figure out how to get over the mountains, and you had the answers all along?" yelled Nova.

"Apparently," said India, edging away from them.

"Give me that book!" said Nova. She rummaged around in India's camping bag, but since she couldn't read titles, she couldn't find the book.

"Give it to me!" yelled Rae. "I can read!"

She joined Nova in rummaging around in the bag. When she found it, she immediately started looking for Avakta. She found Avakta information on pages 38 to 45.

"What does it say?" asked Nova excitedly.

"It says that only a true Vinadala can understand that Avakta's powers are actually..." Rae stopped.

"Actually what?" asked Nova.

"I don't know," answered Rae. "It's all smudged."

"Oops," said India. "I think I might have accidently put Evenherla and Sinxa weed on that page."

"Great," said Rae. "Now we don't know what the secrets of Avakta are."

"We don't need the book," said Nova. "We already have enough information," she said.

"What do you mean?" asked India.

"The book says that true Vinadalas can solve Avakta's problems," said Nova. "We're true Vinadalas, aren't we?" She had learned a little bit about Vinadalas in *The Guide to Ancien Script.*

"It takes more than lots of experience with danger to become a Vinadala," said India. "A true Vinadala has enough powers to be a spirit."

"What powers?" asked Nova.

"The power to change a spirit's mind," answered India.

Nova turned many times to the ore robber. "Could he be a Vinadala?" she thought. "He made Deievede change her mind about pitying him."

Suddenly, Nova had an idea. It might not be a good idea, but it was probably the only idea.

"I think I know what to do," said Nova.

"Really?" asked Rae.

"Yes," said Nova. "All we have to do is change a spirit's mind."

"How?" asked Rae.

"I don't know," answered Nova. "We'd probably have to do what the ore robber did."

"Wait a second," said India. "You're not making me turn into ore."

"I get it," said Rae. "We have to change Landei's mind."

"Landei?" asked India. "Why Landei?"

"Landei knows how to escape the mountains' dangerous qualities," answered Nova. "If we could change her mind about something, we might be able to gather some information."

India still didn't understand, but she went along with Nova and Rae.

"Landei!" yelled Nova.

Landei appeared. She was holding a golden jar.

"What's that jar you're holding?" asked Rae.

"It's the spirit jar," answered Landei. "It holds all the spirits."

"It is very important and delicate, and you must never drop it." Landei gave it to Nova, who just stared at it quizzically.

This was a complete surprise to Rae and India, for right after Landei had told Nova not to drop it, Landei said, "Drop the spirit jar."

Nova dropped the jar and started up the mountain. The jar broke into many small pieces. They climbed up the mountain while Rae, still looking quizzical, watched as a Crivaten appeared. Crivaten looked like a half-lion, half-bird. All three girls started to scream. Even Landei looked worried.

Just then, one of the spirits attacked the Crivaten. As soon as the spirit touched it, he disappeared. The spirits joined together and then separated. They were making the animals disappear. Every time a spirit made an animal disappear, the animal would end up next to the broken spirit jar. The animals were repairing it.

The Crivaten had already produced some Hidaad from his skin. Hidaad was sticky oil. It could be used for many things, but this time it was for repairing the spirit jar.

More and more animals gathered around the spirit jar. They were so intent on the jar, they did not notice the girls or even Landei. The spirits floated in front of the girls as they climbed the mountain. One of the spirits even talked to them. She was bright pink and was one of the only colored spirits in the group.

"Wait a minute!" yelled India. "Aren't you Magenta from *The Extraordinary Five*?"

Rae had no idea what India was talking about. Who were *The Extraordinary Five*? When Rae asked India this, she looked at Rae weirdly.

"Come on, Rae!" she said. "How can you not know *The Extraordinary Five*?"

Rae tried to remember when Matthew may have learned about something called *The Extraordinary Five*, but she finally concluded that he was never smart enough to learn something that advanced.

The other two colored spirits came towards the three girls. One was dark blue, and the other was bright red. The red one seemed to be shielding the blue one. "Pardon the interruption," said the red spirit, "but please take off any shiny items you have on."

"Why?" asked Nova.

"Nova," said India. "If the blue spirit sees anything shiny, she might start exploding things."

"Oh," said Rae. She quickly took off her rose medallion and stuffed it into her pocket.

"Is it safe?" asked the blue spirit, who was slowly coming out from behind the red spirit.

"Yes, Indigo," answered the red spirit.

Indigo glided in front of Magenta and said, "My power has not always been the most useful thing. It has actually been used for only one useful thing that wasn't the most fun."

"It was more fun than Scarlet's," muttered Magenta.

"Hey!" yelled Scarlet, the red spirit. She and Magenta started fighting with each other.

"Guys, stop it!" yelled Indigo. Her efforts were useless. She tried prying the two spirits away from each other, but she only ended up getting poked by both of them.

"I wish Cyan were here," she said. "She was always good at breaking up Magenta and Scarlet's fights."

The name Cyan caught Nova's ear. "Isn't that the spirit who had that weird ESP?" asked Nova.

"Yes," answered Scarlet who had finally stopped fighting with Magenta. "She was the leader of *The Extraordinary Five*."

"She was awesome," said Magenta. "Except when she turned into a weird person named Corellia. I didn't like her much then."

"What happened to her?" asked Rae.

"She went to live with her mother, Fesba, on Celtatza," answered Indigo. "She's now next in line for a royal title because she stopped Calmatza from shrinking and eventually disintegrating."

"With our help," said Magenta.

"Wait," said Rae. "You only named four spirits. Didn't you say there were five?"

"Oh right," said Scarlet. "We forgot Neo."

"You call her Neo?" asked India, who had been stunned to be actually talking to *The Extraordinary Five.*

"We all have nicknames," said Indigo. "Magenta's is Maggie, Cyan's is Cia, Scarlet's is Letta, and Neon's is Neo."

"What about yours?" asked Rae.

"I don't really want to say mine," said Indigo. "It won't make sense to regular humans."

"Just tell us," said India.

"It's Ayo," answered Indigo. "Makes no sense, right?"

"Nope," the three girls answered.

"Well, here we are," said a different voice. Landei stood behind the three spirits and three girls.

She held out the spirit jar, and then every spirit dived in except for Magenta. She said,

"Thank you for everything you have done for us." Then she whispered some sort of name and dived in.

Landei disappeared too. "Good luck," she said.

Nova thought about what Magenta had said about a spirit named Neon. The more she thought about it, the more she remembered about the spirit in the amethyst palace. That spirit had been sort of neon-ish. By the time they got to Sim, Nova knew one thing: the green spirit in the palace was Neon.

India also thought about the name Magenta had said to Landei. She'd been quite sure that it was Landei's name that Magenta said, but the problem was Magenta didn't say anything that sounded like "Landei." She said something like "Jetta." Then India remembered that in the underground passageway Landei had said, "Call me Landei," not, "My name is Landei." By the time they got to Sim, India knew one thing. "Landei" wasn't the spirit's real name.

As for Rae, she mostly thought about her mother and her new home, but she also managed to think of a few other things that made her wonder. How come Nova and Marilyn became servants at the same time she did? How come India looked so much like her? By the time she got to Sim, Rae knew one thing. There was a closer connection between her, Nova, and India than just friendship.

By the time the three girls got to Sim, they noticed one thing: a golden necklace made out of chain.

CHAPTER 20
EVERYTHING IS CLEAR

Nova was the first to see the chain, but India picked it up first. Rae tried to get India to drop it because it looked like it hadn't been touched for at least fifteen years. It had also rolled around in the murky water.

"India, that's gross!" she said.

"No, it's not!" argued India. "It's just old, maybe ancient."

"Didn't you say something about your seeing something gold when you were left here?" asked Nova turning to Rae.

"I saw a golden spear," said Rae. "That's not a golden spear."

"Maybe it wasn't a golden spear," said Nova. "It could've just looked like one."

"Guys!" yelled India who had wandered away to avoid Rae's comments about the necklace being gross.

Nova and Rae ran over to India, who had washed the necklace off in the less murky water.

"It's a status necklace," said India. She pointed out the metal beads. "The diamond-like symbol is the Verlinetasm symbol, the black beads are the number of years of being a Serventsa, the bright orange bead is the Great Thervan Swim, and the golden spear is obviously the royal symbol."

"I don't know Shirley Serventsa," said Nova, "but I don't think she would just leave out her necklace."

"This isn't hers," said India. "It has an orange clip, which means it belongs to a male."

"What color is the female clip?" asked Rae.

"Blue," answered India. "I think it's a lot better."

"Rae!" yelled Nova suddenly. "You did see a golden spear. It was on this necklace."

"No," said Rae. "I saw a full size spear." She didn't want to admit it, but Rae still had doubts that she was a Serventsa. Landei hadn't said anything and neither had any members of *The*

Extraordinary Five. How could she possibly be a Serventsa?

"You probably thought it was a golden spear," said India, "because you were so small."

"Guys," said Nova. She'd wandered off to the other side of Sim. "This is amazing!"

The ground was covered in various jewels, and the path leading up to the palace was solid marble. A few trees were on either side of the path. At the gates, there were tiny potted plants and trees. The whole place was green. It was either made of jade or emerald.

India had seen the Serventsa palace before, but this time it was even more stunning. She walked up toward the gates and examined the architecture. "It looks like the Serventsa palace," she said. Then she started muttering about Borontelle-style architecture.

"India!" said Rae. "Who cares? I'm about to meet my long lost family and become a true Serventsa."

Rae rushed over to the gates, knocking over both India and Nova. Then she froze. Standing at the gates was the Queen herself. She was talking about some sort of event.

"I think the green ones would look best," she said, pulling a green cloth off the wall.

For some strange reason, Rae had a hard time accepting that this was her mother. She looked too straightforward.

"Serventsa Shirley," said a servant. "You have three visitors."

"Open the gates, Mellia," said the Queen. As soon as Shirley Serventsa saw the three girls, she said, "Come inside."

The inside of the Serventsa palace was extraordinary. A crystal chandelier hung from the jade (that's what India had decided it was made of) ceiling. Staircases were everywhere leading to different places, but the most stunning thing of all was all the murals. Giant murals of spirits and humans were painted on the walls. One was of *The Extraordinary Five*.

"I was right!" exclaimed Nova. "The spirit of Laestlan *is* Neon!"

Rae wondered why the Queen hadn't recognized her. All she'd said was, "Come inside."

"The painters got Magenta's nose wrong," Rae said. That didn't get the Queen's attention like she had hoped.

All three girls sat on plush chairs or couches. The servant, Mellia, sat next to Rae, which was a little awkward.

Just then, India remembered. "Rae, where's your medallion?"

Rae's hand flew to her neck, then to her pockets. It was gone!

"India!" yelled Rae.

"Medallion?" asked Mellia, "W-w-what medallion?" She looked like she was trying to hide something.

"Mellia," said the Queen. "Give her the medallion."

Mellia opened her hand. In it was Rae's medallion! "I found it on the floor when these three girls walked in," she said.

"How do you do that?" asked India.

"I'm a descendant of Jenna," answered the Queen. "I'm a half-spirit."

Now that Rae looked at her, she did seem to have a spirit-like attitude.

The Queen stared hard at the medallion and muttered something into a gold jar that Rae soon realized was the spirit jar. Then she dropped the spirit jar like Nova had, and Landei came out. The spirit jar was already starting to re-form.

"Landei!" Rae yelled. "Tell me if I'm a Serventsa!"

She was about to grab the medallion the Queen was holding, but the Queen laid it down on the floor next to the green cloth which had a picture of a rose on it. Her spirit powers kept Rae from trying to grab it again.

"Well, am I?" asked Rae again.

"What do you think?" asked Landei.

Rae really tried to process that. She'd been hoping she was a Serventsa for a while, but no one had said anything except Mrs. Edwards, and she, of course, was Floreian, not Grystallian. It took her a while, but finally she realized that it depended on what she thought, not others.

"Yes!" she answered confidently.

Suddenly, everything went black. She felt like she was falling backwards, but really the palace was leaning forward. When it straightened up again, she was wearing an official status necklace. On it were a golden spear, a black bead, and a blue clip.

IT WAS OFFICIAL.

"Thank you, Landei," said Rae.

"Oh no," said the Queen. "Jenna, you haven't been letting these girls call you Landei."

"I knew it, I knew it!" yelled India. She started yelling, "I knew it!" all around the palace, which made no sense until the Queen explained.

"Landei is only the alias we use for Yellaburgians," she said. "Her real name is Jenna."

"Like the first Serventsa," said Nova. Even she remembered that.

"She is the first Serventsa," said the Queen.

India started bowing down, and Nova and Rae decided to follow, but the spirit had already disappeared.

Rae was about to tell her mother about all the adventures she'd had, but then she noticed India and Nova in their plush chairs. They looked, if it were possible, a little left out.

"Oh," said Rae. "Sorry, guys."

"That's all right," said India who went back to examining the architecture.

The Queen looked hard at India. "What's your name?" she asked.

"India," answered India. "Why?"

"What was your father's name?"

"Mark."

"What's your last name?"

India thought for a moment and then said, "I don't know. It was either Sereta or Seveta."

"I think the name you're searching for is Serventsa," said the Queen.

"Wait – what?" asked India.

"Your father was the King, India," said the Queen.

"Wait," said India, "If my father was the King, that would make you my mother." She thought that was exciting, but then she noticed something even more exciting. "That also makes Rae my sister!"

Then there was lots of shrieking, and after a few minutes the sisters noticed Nova.

The Queen began to stare intently at her too.

"No!" said Nova vehemently. "I am not your daughter and I know it. I have a mother and a twin sister too. My mother's name is Nellida, which is definitely not your name."

"You know what else?" said the Queen. "Nellida's my sister."

That took a while for Nova to figure out. She'd never been good with relations. She knew that if Shirley was Nellida's sister that would make Shirley her aunt, but before she could even work out how Rae and India were related to her, they were jumping on her yelling, "You're our cousin, Nova!"

There was much excitement, which eventually led everyone outside, until India broke up the celebration. "Wait," she said. "Doesn't that mean Marilyn's our cousin too?"

"Oh," said the other two.

"Who's Marilyn?" asked the Queen.

Just then, a loud clatter of footsteps and hooves came behind them.

Nova turned around. "Her," she answered.

It was Marilyn, yet it wasn't Marilyn.

Instead of her usual fancy attire, she wore blue leggings and an oversized sweatshirt with "Grystallian Horse Racing" stitched on it. Her hair was braided, but it wasn't a good braid. It looked like it had been done by someone who braided horse tails. Then Rae realized that if Marilyn had taken the same route, she probably met Andy and Lydia. She was wearing pink shoes, but instead of high heels, they were riding boots.

This surprised the three girls, but what was behind Marilyn surprised them even more. All the servants from Corvate Manor were waving. Some were waving with their hands, but some were waving with pots or pans or whatever else they could find. Behind them were more servants on horses. India was disappointed to see that none of the horses was Jet. There was also a large, red object that was later recognized as a Glider.

From that Glider came Mrs. Corvate, Matthew, and all of her friends, including Oliver Michaels!

As soon as she approached the Queen, she started talking really fast. "I couldn't cut through the stone, so I went all the way back through the underground passageway and piled everyone in my Glider and got here as fast as I could. No interruptions."

"Except for when the horse race judge and his sister distracted you," said Oliver Michaels.

"And when the savage black bird attacked you," said Matthew.

"You two keep out of this!" yelled Mrs. Corvate.

"Victoria," said the Queen, "these girls have nothing to do with you."

"If I had a Sentu for every time I heard that…"

"Victoria, you already have enough Sentus," said the Queen. "Now leave!"

"Make me!" she yelled.

"I will," said Rae. "Mrs. Corvate, imagine a Serventsa were telling you to leave. What would you do?"

"I wouldn't do anything," she answered. "I'm not Grystallian."

"Then face the light of Sorvara!" Rae yelled. She didn't point Sorvara at Mrs. Corvate, but the name, Sorvara, seemed to do the trick.

Mrs. Corvate backed away slowly yelling, "Curse you!" until all of her servants, friends, and horses were back on her Glider.

Only Marilyn stayed. Apparently, she'd decided that she needed to get things straight.

"Nova!" she yelled. "What is going on here?"

Nova took this as an opportunity to face her twin. "Marilyn," she said, "Let me introduce you to my Aunt Shirley."

"Whoa," said Marilyn. "Back up. The Queen is your aunt?"

"Yes," answered Nova. "And Rae and India

are my cousins."

"So?" asked Marilyn.

"We're sisters Marilyn," said Nova.

"So my aunt is Shirley Serventsa?" said Marilyn.

Just then a woman Rae and India had never seen before was running up to them.

"Mother!" Marilyn and Nova yelled.

"Look at you two!" Nellida yelled. "Your clothes!"

"Mother, it doesn't matter," said Nova, "What matters is why you didn't tell us that Shirley Serventsa is your sister."

"Wait," she said, "who told you?"

"Our Aunt Shirley," answered Marilyn.

It was weird, but Marilyn and Nova were agreeing on something. They were both mad at their mother for not telling them.

"It wasn't important," said Nellida.

"Mother," said Marilyn. "We could have lived a royal life. We could have been even more proper than ever. With that much money, we could have even hired an etiquette teacher, but we didn't because you kept one little secret from us."

A loud whinny echoed across the hill. Rae, Nova, and Marilyn thought it was just for effect, but India knew better.

"Jet!!!" she yelled.

The black horse leaped at India. He was certainly in a good mood. Two other horses were galloping behind Jet. India recognized Evan, the horse she had beat in a horse race, and Diamond, Jet's playmate. Lydia was riding Diamond, and Andy was approaching on Evan.

"Guys!" yelled India.

"Hang on!" said Andy. "You owe us a thank you."

"Two thank yous," said Lydia, "One for stalling the Blood Glider and one for returning Jet."

"How did you get here?" asked India.

"We took the passageway through The Outlands," answered Lydia. "On normal horses, it would have taken us twenty years, but Jet helped us along."

"How did you stall Mrs. Corvate?" asked Rae.

"We asked if they wanted free hairdos," said Andy.

"Most of them said no," Lydia said, "but the girl with the brown hair said yes, so we had to – uh, I don't mean to alarm you, but she's standing right there."

"I know," said Nova. "She's my twin sister."

"You're twins?" asked Andy. "You don't look like twins.

"We know," they both answered.

"Andy," said the Queen, "how would you like to judge horse races in Yellaburg, and do sorcery work here?"

"We wouldn't want our sorcery secret to be out," said Andy, "so we'll do one or the other."

"Which one?" asked everyone, including Nellida.

"Sorcery work," they both said.

"Great," said India, "but where will all the horses go?"

"To you," answered Lydia. "We thought about that."

"Great," said the Queen. "I've always wanted a stable, but a certain someone wouldn't let me have one." She glared at Nellida.

"Well, it's not proper," said Nellida.

"Not everything has to proper," said Nova. She held up *The Guide to Ancient Script*. "Have you ever considered studying?"

"Studying?" she exclaimed pushing the book away, "What has happened to you, Nova?"

"Nothing," she answered. "I've never liked being proper. Why would I like it now?"

"For your information," said Nellida, "I did study. I studied the art of trances, so I could talk some sense into you."

"Well, unfortunately, there are some people who know how to break trances," said India, holding up *The Guide to Ancient Arts*.

"Come on, Nellida," said the Queen. "Forget about being proper and start thinking about royal life. You'll all be living with me."

The idea made Rae excited. She ran towards the doors, but just before entering, she looked back on all the adventures she'd had and what might come next.

As a Serventsa, you never have a boring moment.

EPILOGUE

If you think about me being a Serventsa for a long time, you might realize it's not really that proper, like Marilyn said. Oh, by the way, it's me, Rae, talking.

I think the right way to end this adventure is to tell you what royal life is like for us.

India seems happy. She's always riding or swimming. She tells me it's a great way to spend time and train for the Great Thervan Swim, which her father did.

She spends a lot of time at the spirit jar talking to members of *The Extraordinary Five*. She has officially refused to wear anything shiny for Indigo's sake. She sometimes goes down to Laestlan to talk with Neon. Since she's got powers against Laestlan, she claims that she can go there whenever she wants.

Nova is pretty much the "brainiac" of my family. She does a lot of studying, and even knows more than India about Jenna, who she's come to love.

She also spends a lot of time at the spirit jar, which was hard at first, since India also wants to be there, but now we have a schedule for spirit jar meetings. She's even figured out why Indigo's nickname is Ayo, but she won't tell us.

Marilyn isn't doing much. She spent twenty Sentus on an etiquette tutor, but other than that, she tries to make herself look fashionable. Her hair took a while to comb out after the braid incident. She now only does her hair herself.

She complains all the time about how there is no Spirit of Fashion. I tried to ask her what the Spirit of Fashion would be named, which only made it worse. Now she has six scrolls of possible names. "Marilyn" is one of them.

As for me, I'm looking around my new home. I don't have to a share room with anyone, which is a relief. I like being a Serventsa. I love using Sorvara and having the ability to use it, but if you're thinking that I'm the only one with powers, think again.

Next up: *THE THREE MASKS*

GLOSSARY

Alveran: A mountain that erupts Grysetsa. (AHL-ver-an)

Avakta: A jungle mountain. (A-VAHK-ta)

Borontelle-style: A type of architecture commonly used for palaces. (Bor-ON-tel)

Calmatza: The planet of the humans. (Cal-MAWT-sa)

Celtatza: The planet of the spirits where Fesba and Deievede live. (Sel-TAT-sa)

Crivaten: A half-lion half-bird that often roams the jungles of Avakta. (CRI-vuh-ten)

Deievede: The spirit of equality, daughter of Celtatza, and the queen of the spirits. (dei-EI-ve-dee)

Evenherla: A white plant that will turn red when Sinxa weed wears off. (even-HAIR-la)

Fectaria: A mountain that is not as high as it looks. (Fek-TAIR-ee-a)

Fesba: The spirit of human creation and the mother of The Extraordinary Five. (FEZ-ba)

Florei: A town in between Yellaburg and Grystall. (flor-AY)

Grysetsa: A spirit summoning liquid. (Gri-SET-sa)

Grystall: A town on the East side of Calmatza. (GRI-stall)

Hidaad: The sticky oil from a Crivaten's skin. It can be used for many different purposes. (HEE-dawd)

Laestlan: A mountain with an amethyst palace. (LAYST-lahn)

Landei: The alias name for Jenna, the first Serventsa. (LAHN-day)

Meianrus: The spirit of evil and the daughter of Celtatza.

Ofortan: A mountain with dangerously high altitude. (Oh-FORT-tahn)

Sentu: Calmatzian currency. (SEN-too)

Serventsa: A royal of Grystall. (Sir-VENT-suh)

Sim: A very small hilltop by the Serventsa palace. (SEEM)

Sinxa weed: Stalks of a yellowish plant that enable you to talk and breathe underwater. (SIN-ksa)

Telenemest: A mountain that looks like a ball of flames. (Tel-LANE-mest)

The Outlands: Wide grassland that takes up the side of Calmatza that doesn't have towns. Part of it sticks into Florei.

Thervan: A mountain that looks like it is underwater, but is really floating. (THER-vahn)

Thervan Swim: A swimming race that takes place in the middle of July.

Verlinetasem: A lost legend. (Ver-LINE-a-taz-em)

Vestale: Loosely translates from Grystallian, as Mile. (VES-tel)

Vinadala: A person who has experience with danger and has extreme power with the help of tools. (Vin-a DAHL-a)

Yellaburg: A town on the West side of Calmatza. (YELL-uh-berg)

ABOUT THE AUTHOR

Elisa Johnson is a ten-year-old girl who lives in the Pacific Northwest. She started *The Rose* in 2013 and finished it on January 25, 2015.

The Rose is the beginning to Elisa's *Calmatza Series*, which will include nine other books. She is also working on a *Celtatza Series*, which focuses on spirits and half-spirits and a movie called *Temple Run,* which is based on the video game.

She plans to set many of her stories in Calmatza or Celtatza.

All proceeds from the sale of The Rose go toward The Mandalay Project, a program that supports schools in need and mobile libraries in Mandalay, Myanmar.

Cover photo by Katy von Brandenfels

The Mandalay Project: Background

I went to Myanmar for the first time in 2012 when I was in 1st grade. On that trip, our guide, John, helped us visit a school outside the city of Mandalay. It was easy to see how much the school needed, and I knew I wanted to help. When I returned home, I founded The Mandalay Project and began raising money to buy school supplies. John helped me to buy and deliver text books, pencils, school bags and new uniforms to the school I had visited. I also had enough money to build a mobile library that travels around to different schools in need. Last summer, my family traveled back to Myanmar to visit the school and mobile library. I am now fundraising again to support more mobile libraries and supplies for the school. I am giving all the royalties I make from The Rose to The Mandalay Project.

Elisa Johnson, January 2016

35934264R00108

Made in the USA
San Bernardino, CA
08 July 2016